CAPTIVES OF THE CANYON

FRONTIER BRIDES, BOOK 4

Colleen L. Reece

CHIVERS

British Library Cataloguing in Publication Data available

This Large Print edition published by AudioGO Ltd, Bath, 2013.
Published by arrangement with the Author

U.K. Hardcover   ISBN   978 1 4458 2675 2
U.K. Softcover   ISBN   978 1 4458 2678 3

Scripture quotations are taken from the King James Version of the Bible.

Printed and bound in Great Britain by
MPG Books Group Limited

AUTHOR'S NOTE

The legends concerning Dead Horse Point and Dead Horse Canyon are real although unproved. Due to a lack of actual dates other than vague references to "just before the turn of the century," etc., I have taken literary license and fitted these legendary events into the time frame of my novel while remaining as accurate as possible to what I learned in researching the area.

Colleen L. Reece

CHAPTER 1

Footsore and weary, Andy Cullen paused in the endless pursuit of his chestnut mare, Chinquapin, and, with disfavor, surveyed the world around him. "Why'd I ever leave the Double J ranch?" he complained to a buzzard sailing overhead, bent on its grisly mission. Yet even his sour mood couldn't erase the joy of living that evidenced itself in sparkling brown eyes and a grin like the crack in a cheap watermelon. A lock of hair, darkened by sweat from its normal, ripe corn color, dangled over his forehead. Andy shoved it back under his Stetson, then mopped his hot face with a bright red neckerchief and eyed the crowding red-rock walls that towered above him and offered a million hiding places for a frightened horse. "Chinq, at least they didn't get you." He limped to a nearby boulder the size of a house and leaned against it, glad for the shade.

"Lord, if You're really the way Columbine and Smokey believe, I could sure use a hand. This southeastern Utah ain't no place for a cowpoke on foot a million miles from nowhere. No water. No canteen. Nothing but red and orange rocks." His gaze traveled across the strange, broken land. Great stone arches loomed above him. Formations that looked like petrified giants kept everlasting vigil. Massive rocks that resembled pictures of great cathedrals he'd once seen stood like sentinels. Andy shuddered. Alone, hungry, and thirsty, they posed a serious threat — not only to his quest but to his life.

"I reckon You help those who help themselves," he muttered and straightened. High-heeled boots raised him taller than his five feet, nine inches. He stretched muscled arms. Every sinew in his body ached. Lean, stripling, seasoned, the unaccustomed walking that all riders hated had taken its toll, and Chinq had been missing only since last night.

Andy made a disgusted sound. How could he have been so careless? On the other hand, who'd expect any self-respecting outlaw band to be in a forsaken place like this? His cheerful mouth set in a straight line. "I must be crazy, leaving a good job to chase wild horses. Wild horse, to be exact. I never should have listened to all the stories about Sheik. If I hadn't, I'd be home where I belong."

He thought wistfully of the Double J ranch near Flagstaff. Of Smokey Travis, Columbine Ames, now Mrs. Smokey, and the exasperating but lovable Jim Perkins with his favorite expression, "Snappin' crocodiles." Of Joel, the boy preacher, and all the others. Andy had been welcomed and made part of the Double J family after helping Columbine escape her iron-willed father the previous, fateful summer of 1891.

Most of all he remembered the showdown between Smokey and Zeke Stockton, Columbine's stepfather, who wanted to marry her. Even now his heart broke into a gallop at the memory. When Zeke called Smokey out, Smokey had refused to fight him. Instead, he had chosen to face the inevitable scorn of the range and be branded a coward rather than kill someone, even for Colley's sake.

Andy's big grin spread. If he lived to be older than the red-rock castles around him, he'd never forget his dark-haired, dark-eyed cowboy friend standing in front of the Double J hours after his wedding, his frail, white-clad bride on his arm. Neither would he forget Zeke's charge like an angry bull and what had followed.

"Coward! Skunk! Will you get a gun?" Zeke had bellowed.

"No." Smokey didn't give an inch.

"I'd never have figured you for a yellow-belly. Is it 'cause I'm her daddy?" Zeke stood with his cocked Colt aimed directly at Smokey's heart.

A smile creased Smokey's face. "Yesterday I'd have shot you an' felt bad for Columbine. Now I won't. I turned my life over to God last night, an' He don't hold with killing, no matter what."

A rush of flying feet and Columbine's bell-like voice said, "Father, I love him. The same way you loved Mother and she loved you." That brought Zeke down like a swooping eagle felled with a bullet. To the amazement of all present, he backed off and rode away.

Nothing in Andy's life had impressed him so much as seeing his pard face death rather than go back on his newly found Trailmate. Now Andy soliloquized, "Maybe someday, after I catch Sheik, I'll go back. They said I'll always have a job waiting." He pictured the ranch in his mind. Rolling hills that leveled off in mesas, then climbed until they became distant mountains. Sweet-smelling pine and cedar. Laughter and lighted windows. A pang went through him. The Double J stood for home, the only one he'd known since his parents died and, as a young boy, he had to make it on his own. It seemed incredible that he had ridden away.

"No use pretending," he said ruefully. "Once I turned nineteen in January and stories about Sheik came down from range gossip, I knew I had to track him."

That had been just a few months ago. Andy lounged in the bunkhouse during stormy weather, rode the range when it lifted, but his mind soared north and east. Chinquapin, the mare he'd been given, steadily served his needs and proved herself a satisfying companion. But to own Sheik, the legendary black stallion who fully lived up to his name by stealing every mare possible and driving would-be leaders from his band in fierce battle that boded no good for challengers! Excitement flowed through Andy's veins at the very thought. Couldn't he just see himself riding into the corral on Sheik, hand tamed and glistening ebony!

Reality interrupted his daydreams. "How can it be so hot for spring?" he mumbled. "Summer must be awful." He sighed and increased his pace. "Let's see. I must be a good fifteen miles from Moab. I can't be

11

sure with all these twists and turns. Lord, I reckon You're the only one who knows where I am for sure."

Trailwise, he considered his choices. Trying to travel at night in this unfamiliar country meant the chance of a slip or fall, possibly a broken leg. "Ump-umm." Working his way out of his predicament by day and without water offered an equally unalluring prospect. Best thing to do would be to travel in late afternoon, early evening, and early morning, and hole up during the hottest part of the day. He thought longingly of his well-stocked pack. He'd replenished his supplies in Moab. Now they merrily rode in outlaw saddlebags.

"At least they didn't get Chinq," he gloated. Andy never hobbled her at night; she liked to nuzzle the oats he carried or graze close by when she could find grass.

The other night, though, Andy had been caught off guard. He didn't hear soft footfalls until just before a voice ordered, "Hands up!" When he hesitated, a bullet whistled past his left ear, too close for comfort. His hands shot skyward. Chinq snorted and leaped at the same moment. Her strong shoulder knocked against one of the three dark figures approaching Andy's fire, and a second mighty bound plunged her from the circle of light into blackness.

A volley of yells shattered the crisp night air. A loud "Haw-haw" came from one of the intruders as the fallen one scrambled to his feet and rubbed his arm and shoulder.

"Got any money?" the voice he'd heard earlier asked.

"Not much." Andy tried honesty. "Spent most of it at Moab on supplies." He bit his lip. Of all the stupid remarks, that had to be the worst.

"Good. We'll take them. Traveling men like us can always use more grub." The thieves stepped forward. All that showed between pulled-down hats and pulled-up bandannas were glittering eyes that clearly warned him not to argue. He silently watched them gather his stores, hoping they wouldn't notice Chinq's saddlebags hanging from a small rock outcropping nearby. They contained food he'd need to get back to Moab.

"Hey, Boss, lookee here," one called. He dangled the saddlebags from his hand, and by the flickering campfire light, Andy saw the gleam in his shaded eyes. Strange eyes, almost colorless. If he saw them again, Andy felt he would recognize those eyes.

"What're you doing out here anyway?"

Again Andy resorted to total honesty.

13

"Tracking Sheik."

"Whew!" The man with the odd eyes let out a low whistle.

"You've sure got the right bait," the outlaw who'd taken charge admitted. "What I saw of that mare will be mighty appealing to Sheik, the old robber." He laughed, a surprisingly pleasant sound. "But my pard here got a closer look than I did." He ignored the victim of Chinq's flight when he continued, "You'll find your mare in a day or two if Sheik don't find her first."

For a moment, Andy forgot his loss of supplies and eagerly asked, "Have you seen the stallion and his band lately?"

The masked man shook his head. "Naw. But I heard a few days ago that some rancher was madder than a sore-footed wildcat 'cause Sheik had stolen a couple of his mares." With a swift motion, he turned. "We don't have time to gab, Mister. Thanks for the grub." He raised his revolver and placed a well-aimed shot over Andy's right shoulder. "Don't think about tracking us instead of the stallion." He and his men melted into the dark shadows but not until Andy had caught an unwilling look of admiration in the other's eyes when Andy didn't flinch at the shot.

"Funny galoot," Andy muttered at the

memory and walked on in the direction that Chinq's faint tracks led. "If he weren't a miserable thief, I could like the feller. Sure had a sense of humor." He bent his keen gaze to the trail. Here and there, it crossed solid rock and had left no impression. Andy faithfully picked it up again wherever sand had drifted down, yet, by the time darkness had come, he hadn't found his horse. Neither had he seen a jackrabbit, prairie dog, or even a lizard. No supper tonight. He tightened his belt a notch, broke off a few branches from a nearby stunted greasewood, and built a small fire to ward off the growing chill. His bedroll had gone the way of his grub, so he dozed, fed his blaze, and spent a miserable night. Sometime after two o'clock, according to the battered pocket watch he carried, he drifted into an uneasy sleep.

A sound in the night brought him bolt upright. His fire had dwindled and cast only a feeble light. Something in the hovering shadows moved. Andy swallowed and reached for his Colt. "Who's there?"

Nothing answered, but again something moved just beyond the fire's glow.

"Come out, or I'll shoot," he sharply ordered. At the same time, he sprang to his feet and dove to one side, then rolled away from the light into the protective cover of night. If the outlaws had come back, it would be to kill. They knew he had no horse or food and had seemed satisfied as to his state of finances, not bothering to search. They had actually been quite gentlemanly, as robbers go.

Andy's irrepressible grin flashed even while he slithered farther from the fire. The next moment, a complaining whinny sent him into gales of laughter. "Stampeded," he choked when he could speak. "Held up by my own horse!" He stood and crossed to Chinquapin, tossing extra greasewood branches on the fire as he went. "You old fraud. What's the idea of sneaking back here in the middle of the night?" He stroked her tangled mane. His hand felt gritty and showed red dust in the firelight. "A sorry mess you are, but I'll tell the world if I ain't glad to see you."

Chinquapin rubbed her head against his shoulder and moved restlessly.

"Sorry, Girl. No feed for either of us, but tomorrow we'll go into Moab. I still have enough money to get us fed up. May have to look for a job soon, though. I hadn't counted on losing our supplies and my bedroll."

■ ■ ■ ■

True to his word, by daylight Andy and Chinq were ready to leave. First he made a trip back to the scene of the robbery. The men had left the cowboy's heavy saddle, and he certainly hadn't wanted to pack it in his search for Chinquapin. Unwilling to put saddle to bare horsehide, Andy used his jacket as a saddle blanket. The corners of his mouth turned down. Smokey and Jim Perkins had given him that blanket for Christmas. "One thing about it," he promised Chinq. "If I see that blanket, I'll know who stole our outfit. Columbine put a tiny *A* for Andy in one corner." He brightened at the thought. Sooner or later, even outlaws had to ride into towns and ranches to stock up. Usually they passed themselves off as strangers riding through or as respectable cowhands, unless they were downright killers, and he had a feeling these men weren't. They could have shot him, dumped his body in a canyon, and never feared being caught in this contorted place. If his remains were ever discovered, the buzzards and coyotes wouldn't have left enough to recognize who it was.

The ugly idea sent sweat to Andy's forehead. "Lord, I guess since I had to meet rustlers or outlaws or whatever they are, I'd better be thankful they weren't any worse." He paused. "Maybe it ain't too respectful talking to You like this, but Smokey says You're a Trailmate, and that's how I'd talk to my best pard." Saying it out loud kind of made it sound better. Andy whistled a cheerful melody and turned Chinq in the direction he hoped Moab lay.

Alas for his plans! When the sun was high in the sky, he found they'd been traveling off course. "Oh, no. That means more hungry, thirsty miles," he told Chinq. "Sorry. I'll make up for it when we get to town."

Once out of the canyon country, they made good time. Andy's growling stomach reminded him how long it had been since supper the other night. Chinq, powerful as she was, was drooping by the time they reached Moab and the livery stable. With the range appreciation of a horse that becomes comrade as well, Andy allowed no one to care for the mare but himself. He fed and watered her, then brushed her chestnut coat to its usual gleam before striding down the wide and dusty main street to a small but excellent cafe. Forty-five minutes later, filled to the brim with tender beefsteak, fried potatoes, too many hot buttered biscuits to count, and side dishes of three vegetables followed by two huge slabs of apple pie, he leaned back and considered his next move.

A conversation at the next table caught his attention. He glanced that way. Four men sat with elbows on the red-checked tablecloth. The one facing Andy looked like he'd just won a bulldogging contest at an annual Fourth of July doings.

"I tell you, it can be done. We'll herd Sheik and his band onto the rock point that overlooks Dead Horse Canyon, barricade it, and have him where we want him."

Andy felt like he'd just swallowed a boulder. Corral *his* wild stallion? Never! He started to rise, decided to be cautious, and motioned for more coffee. Nursing it would give him a good reason to linger and overhear more.

"How come they call it Dead Horse Canyon, anyway?" the broad-shouldered man who sat with his back to Andy demanded.

"There's a rock just below the point that looks like a horse lying on its side. White sandstone. Legend says it's a caveman's horse that fell off a cliff and got petrified."

"I heard it's because someone found a

horse drowned in a deep pothole, probably trying to get a drink," another put in. "The sides were too steep to climb out."

The fourth man pounded the table with his fist. "Who cares? What's important is whether it will work."

"It'll work, all right." The first speaker sounded positive. "Mustang herds run wild all over the mesas out there. The promontory's a natural corral, I tell you. The only way on or off it is a thirty-yard-wide neck of land. We can fence it, rope and break the good stock, and either keep them or sell them. There's big money in selling to eastern markets."

"What about the culls, the broomtails?"

"Open the gate. They're smart enough to find their way off the point, ain't they?"

"If we go ahead, one thing's understood." The broad-shouldered man whose face Andy couldn't see spoke clearly and slowly. "If we succeed with this, Sheik's mine. I'll keep him for breeding and get rich."

"No doubt about it," one of his companions drawled. "That stallion's said to be half pure Arabian and half wild stallion. His daddy done stole his mama from George Allen. George sure hated to lose her. Said she was the best mare he ever had."

"Wonder what he'd pay to get Sheik, with

the mare to boot? By the way, what happened to Sheik's sire?"

Excitement faded from the first speaker's eyes. "A wild horse hunter roped him, half broke him, and sold him to a rancher who beat the horse and made a killer out of him. One day they found the rancher about dead, stomped." Anger filled his face. "Y'know how they put a price on outlaws' heads? Well, they did the same with that wonderful horse. After the stallion tore down the corral and escaped, some greedy snake killed the stallion so's he could collect the reward."

Andy heard the indignation in the little ripple of protest that ran around the table. Although not bloodthirsty, he could agree to a point when the broad-shouldered man viciously snapped, "Served the rancher right. Might as well kill a mustang as beat him." He shoved back his chair and stood; the others followed. Throwing money on the table, they noisily marched out, leaving Andy shaken.

He paid his bill and ambled outside. All the money he had left must go for supplies. No sleeping in a real bed tonight. He could ride out of town and find a ranch that would give him a place to sleep and breakfast, the usual range hospitality. He shook his head. Chinq needed rest, and he had too much to think about to sleep well. The night promised to be clear, so he headed for the same store where he'd stocked up just days before and entered.

"Back so soon?" The proprietor behind the counter laden with everything from harness to dry goods, canned goods to candy, grinned. "What'd you do, lose your grub?"

"How did you know?" Andy asked.

The deadly words and menacing step that Andy took forward turned the storekeeper's face doughy. "Why, I'm just funnin', Mister," he said.

Andy relaxed and grinned sheepishly. Obviously, the man knew nothing. "Sorry. Three bad men held me up."

Color seeped back into the pasty face. "Sorry to hear it. What can I do for you?"

Andy chose sparingly: flour, bacon, saddle blanket, bedroll.

"Mighty lucky you had some of your money well hid," the proprietor said admiringly.

Andy didn't explain. He still had trouble figuring out why the thieves hadn't made him fork over everything. He merely nodded, waited until the friendly man put everything in an old flour sack, then paid him and walked out, nearly broke but secretly thankful. Strange, how things worked out.

"Might say those scoundrels actually did me a favor," he mumbled. "If they hadn't robbed me, I wouldn't be back in Moab and know Sheik's whereabouts and what those four men aim to do."

A frown marred his smooth forehead. He had to get to Sheik before the quartet carried through their plan, or all his months of wandering and hardship meant nothing.

That night Andy lay snug and warm on a straw bed. The livery stable owner had agreed he could sleep there for two bits extra. Andy dug deep in his jeans and paid him for the night's lodging plus Chinq's board bill. "I'll be leaving early," he casually said. "Might as well square up now."

"Okay by me, Sonny." The old man grinned. His keen eyes beneath shaggy brows observed his customer until Andy knew that, if he had anything to hide, he wouldn't want this man quizzing him. He hastily bid the older man good night and set about mounding hay into a mattress. He slept soundly after the last two nights of sketchy rest, and his brain awakened him to the sun peeping over the eastern horizon. Before Moab had begun to stir, man and beast had quietly left town.

Once out of sight of possible curious watchers, Andy turned Chinq north and west — straight toward the place called Dead Horse Point. Thirty-some miles lay between him and his destination, and a sense of urgency whispered in his ear, *Hurry, hurry.* Chinq responded to his commands and swung into her easy, tireless stride, which covered the miles and left her rider free to cogitate his next moves.

CHAPTER 2

When Andy Cullen stood on Dead Horse Point and gazed into the canyon below, he knew he would never forget it. Two thousand feet of red, orange, and rust cliffs, purple-shadowed by late evening, lay at his feet and ended in the curving Colorado River below. Tortuous, twisting, ever cutting, to Andy's trained eyes, it looked a little wider than a rusty ribbon. He had stood on the south rim of the Grand Canyon in Arizona Territory and gazed at the same river miles south and west. Now he experienced the identical sense of awe, of his own smallness compared with the greatness of a God who created such untamed beauty.

He turned away, only to swing back and look again. In those few seconds, the canyon's face had mysteriously changed. Pockets of mist hovered, mercifully disguising the raw, wounded cliffs, softening and draping them until a mere beholder dwindled in proportion to their might.

A verse that Joel, the boy preacher, once quoted in a sermon about David, the shepherd boy who became king, came to mind. *The fool hath said in his heart, There is no God.* Andy shook his head. No man could stand where he stood, see what he saw, without knowing how big a fool one must be to believe such a lie. He bared his head with its shock of ripe corn hair, held his Stetson in one hand, and watched until lengthening shadows warned of the need to make camp. Yet the spell of the canyon, the stirrings within him to know its Creator better, overrode the excitement of his wild horse chase.

Morning brought a whole new set of shifting shadows, and again the canyon's face lay changed and appealing. Andy found himself reluctant to ride on, even though he had learned what he wanted to know. The four men in the Moab cafe had been right. The promontory, reached only by that neck of land, offered the finest natural corral in the world once a high fence closed off its entrance behind a band of horses.

"Ump-umm," Andy told Chinq. His brown eyes glistened. "There ain't no man alive who can build a fence high enough to hold Sheik unless he's been tamed." A thrill of pure joy went through him. Every story of the racing black stallion that Andy had unearthed in his search for him made Andy more determined to catch, tame, and own the half-Arabian horse. His quick mind seized on a name used in the Moab cafe. Allen, George Allen. He wrinkled his forehead in concentration and saddled Chinquapin. "I've heard of him, old girl. Runs a big spread near Moab. What's the name of it? Lazy A, Bar A, no . . . Rocking A. That's it." With the toe of his boot, he traced an A in the dust. "If we don't find Sheik before our supplies give out, we'll head for the Rocking A and have a little confab with Mr. Allen. If it ain't too late for spring roundup, he can probably use an extra hand. We're pretty good shakes at cutting and branding, aren't we, Chinq?" A solemn look settled over Andy's merry face. Taking time out to earn money to restock their supplies meant that much time away from tracking Sheik and his band. In the meantime, the Moab quartet would be moving ahead with their plan to fence off the promontory.

He shook off forbidding thoughts, carefully stamped out the remains of his breakfast fire, and stretched his lithe body in a sky-reaching move, then vaulted to Chinquapin's back, young, alive, and hopeful.

The hope ran swift and hot in his veins for a few days, then petered out along with the horse tracks he'd been following. The wily Sheik obviously knew every escape trick recognized by pursuers, and then some. Just when Andy felt he'd catch the band the next day, a stretch of solid rock with tracks that led to the edge and disappeared stopped him short. "Where . . . ?" He peered down, squinted, and looked across the steep expanse of sheer rock. Horses couldn't traverse that, could they? Especially unshod horses, even Sheik. It took Andy's best skills to discover an innocent-looking narrow side trail — one of a dozen like it — with signs of his quarry. "Horse droppings," he exulted. He climbed down from the saddle and examined them. "Yippee! Still fresh." Fired with new enthusiasm, he led Chinq onto the trail barely wide enough for a horse and squeezed between high, jagged rocks. "I wouldn't bring you in here if other horses hadn't come first," he assured his suddenly skittish mare. "There has to be a wide place to turn around, or Sheik wouldn't have brought his band here."

Chinquapin snorted, and Andy laughed. She sounded totally disgusted at the

cramped conditions. "If you were Jim Perkins, right now you'd be bellyaching and
saying, 'Snappin' crocodiles, where are we
goin'?' " he teased.

Chinq shook her head but obediently followed. A right-angle turn took some coaxing before the mare trotted on behind him.
How on earth had Sheik discovered the trail
in the first place?

"I'll just bet he was being chased. Or
maybe his father before him knew the
place." He led Chinquapin over a few fallen
rocks and shuddered. One good rumbling
of the earth would send a shower of boulders and trap any living creatures between
the walls that bordered the trail.

Another turn, this time to the left, and —

"My word!" Andy stopped so suddenly
that the chestnut mare bumped into him.
The trail and rock walls ended simulta-
neously. A small green valley with red-rock
cliffs surrounding it lay ahead, narrow
where he stood, widening for about a mile
before reaching the sheltering cliffs. A
stream ran through it. Lush green grass
covered the valley floor, and the rotting
remains of an old cabin leaned tipsily
beneath the shade of an enormous cottonwood. They vaguely impressed themselves
on Andy's mind in his sweeping, lightning

glance but slipped into unimportance when he focused his gaze on the far end of the box canyon. A herd of horses stood grazing. Mares, colts, yearlings.

Andy sucked in his breath and strained his eyes to see. His heartbeat quickened. "Where's Sheik?"

Chinquapin tossed her head and neighed. With uncharacteristic independence, she pranced from behind her master and galloped down the valley toward her own kind.

"Chinq!" Andy yelled, more amused than angry.

She ignored him and raced on.

"Great. We've tracked them all this way, are nearly out of grub, and Sheik ain't around. Chinq deserts me, and here I stand like one of them dummies in a store window." Andy shook his head and started forward. His mare had reached the band now. A few of the horses raised their heads; others went on grazing. One old mare nipped at the newcomer's flanks, and Chinquapin danced away, whinnying a protest.

Suddenly tired by disappointment as well as the long chase, Andy headed down the valley. "It ain't reasonable for this band of horses to be here without a stallion," he muttered. "Who led them in here, anyway?" His practiced gaze checked out the colts and yearlings. Not a horse there looked capable of heading up a band like this one. There had to be a stallion with the herd, but where was he?

The horrid scream of a horse in mortal terror split the peace of the quiet valley. Andy's heart leaped until he could barely swallow. He'd heard such screams before, not often, thankfully. Fear lent speed to his booted feet. He veered off to the left, splashed across the surprisingly deep stream and through a clump of screening cottonwoods, aware of pounding hooves behind him as the herd responded to the cry.

A heartrending sight met him when he stopped on the other side of the cottonwoods. A black stallion fought desperately to free himself from a tumble of rocks at the foot of a cliff. Half-buried, his powerful body lunged against the imprisoning boulders that trapped him. Andy saw a dusty trail winding up the red mountain, no wider than the one on which he'd come. So it wasn't a box canyon after all. The trail provided an alternate way out.

"Wrong," he whispered. "No man or beast will get out that way. Sheik — it has to be him — got caught partway up and was swept down." He longed to rush forward but restrained himself. "God, what can I

31

do? If he thrashes around, he's going to either break his legs or kill himself." Tears dimmed his eyes at the sight of the magnificent, losing fight. The black screamed again. Dark shadows blotted out the sun — buzzards, gliding down to perch on nearby rocks and wait.

"No!" Andy could not stand by and see Sheik become buzzard bait. He instinctively reached for his Colt and drew and cocked it. The greatest gift he could give Sheik was instant death. He raised the revolver, aimed. His hand shook until he couldn't steady it. Andy sobbed, all his boyish love for the legendary horse flowing forth in renunciation of his dream. "Good-bye, Sheik."

He took a deep breath and held it. His arm stilled. In a second he would pull the trigger and pray for the first bullet to reach the stallion's brain. If he missed, could he force himself to fire again?

Before Andy could squeeze the trigger, a cold nose poked itself over his left shoulder and against his cheek. Distracted, Andy hesitated and glanced at Chinquapin. She lipped his ear, then stepped away. He tore his gaze from her and glanced back at the black, whose struggles looked feebler, slower. Again he steadied the revolver.

A clatter of hooves. A chestnut mare moving into his vision. "What's going on?" Andy's unshaven, lower jaw dropped. Chinquapin had again deserted, this time to pick her way across the fallen rock until she reached the trapped stallion. Like a slave to her master, she made a beeline to him and stopped only feet away.

"Chinq, come back!"

Ba–ack . . . ba–ack . . . came the echoes from the red cliffs.

"Chinq!" Andy implored and sprinted toward her. The cliffside had slid once. It could slide again, trapping her as well as Sheik. Frantically, Andy prayed, "Lord, You made these critters. Please, help me save them." He considered and rejected a dozen ideas. By the time he could remove the rocks, Sheik would be gashed and weakened from blood loss, if it were not already too late. Every ounce of strength would go into fighting man, his long-held foe, should Andy get close. Just now, Sheik lay still, watching Chinquapin — and her master. The cowboy knew it would not last long, yet his only hope rested in that stillness.

"Lord?"

Like a bolt of lightning, a bit of range lore lunged into his consciousness. No one on the Double J ever considered using it; too dangerous, the older hands said. But some wild horse tamers practiced a method hated by most ranchers. They creased a horse with a bullet, not shooting to kill but to stun. By the time horses regained their senses, they had been securely tied.

Desperate men take desperate chances. With a quick prayer, Andy once more raised his revolver. If the bullet went too deep, it meant the end of Sheik's suffering. If not . . . He scarcely let himself hope.

Andy fired. *Spang.* The sound of the shot ricocheted back and forth across the valley, bounced off the walls, and repeated itself a hundred times. The herd, who had crowded close to its fallen leader, reared, snorted, and raced away. All but Chinquapin, who stood looking down at the motionless stallion with great eyes.

Andy leaped toward the horses. If the shot had grazed as he intended, he had no time to lose. He whooped with joy when he saw the rise and fall of breath that showed the stallion hadn't been killed. "Thanks, Pard," he shouted and attacked the boulders with all his might, glad for the muscle and bone and sinew made hard by clean living and excruciating work. Rock after rock he tossed aside, until he'd freed Sheik's front feet. In a twinkling, he tied them together. "Can't take a chance on his coming to and striking out," he told Chinquapin, who had crowded closer to watch. He also blindfolded Sheik with his bandanna.

A shudder went through him when he saw the torn flesh on the black's flanks, but he couldn't stop with his digging. A ripple of movement through Sheik's frame warned that the effect of the bullet had almost worn off. With a last desperate effort, Andy tackled the remaining rocks and firmly secured the wounded horse's back feet.

"Just in time." He mopped his sweaty face. Sheik's body shook with a convulsion that would have brought him to his feet if he hadn't lain bound. He jerked his head up as far as he could and struggled to stand. Another scream of frustration rent the air.

"It's all right, Boy. You've been hurt, and I helped you. Take it easy. I ain't going to hurt you," Andy soothed.

He might as well have spit against the wind for all the good it did in calming the stallion. Sheik bared his teeth, emitted another full-throated scream, and tried to reach his captor in a mighty bite.

Andy laughed. "I don't blame you. If somebody shot at me and I came to tied like a bulldogged steer, I'd holler, too. Take all the time you need getting used to me. We ain't going anywhere. There's water

35

here, and I'll bet there's game. You and me and Chinquapin are going to get to be real good friends before we leave this hideout of yours."

One of the buzzards let out a squawk, flapped its wings, and flew off. The others followed. Andy's mirth changed to a grim gladness. "No meal for you here, scavengers." He strode to Chinquapin, led her back near the dilapidated shack, and peered inside. "Ugh. Unless it pours, I'll stay outside." Deft hands unpacked supplies, threw off the saddle and new saddle blanket. Free of her burden, Chinquapin danced a bit, then to her owner's surprise, headed back to the fallen stallion.

"Well, found yourself a sweetheart, have you?" Andy grinned and rummaged in his saddlebags. He brought forth soap, a soft cloth, and the extra hackamore he packed for just such an occasion as this. No better time to get it on the black than when he lay helpless. Even so, it took all his strength to avoid the big, vicious teeth and wild turnings of Sheik's magnificent head long enough to get him bridled. He tightened the long loop that served in place of a bit over the stallion's nose. Time enough for that later. Right now, all he wanted to do was to get Sheik used to him and tend to his torn flesh.

It took a full hour to wash the wounds and involved Chinquapin's help in getting the stallion on his feet. Andy loosened the sturdy ropes around Sheik's legs enough to force him to hobble to the creek at the end of a lasso wound around the chestnut mare's saddle horn. "Hold him fast," Andy ordered. Using a cooking pan scoured clean with red sand from the creek bottom, Andy poured stream after stream of water over the black, rejoicing in its chill. His keen gaze had discovered where it gushed from the rocky earth near the base of a cliff. It could be the mouth of one of the many southwestern streams that seemingly vanished into nowhere, then reappeared in the unlikeliest places.

"There, old boy. I've done what I can." Andy eyed the drenched horse, then ordered Chinquapin to haul him out. "Thanks, Lord. No broken legs. He's not even limping; just hating and fighting the ropes. He couldn't have lost all that much blood, either, or he wouldn't have the stamina to keep struggling. Glad he stayed a little dazed until the worst of it got over."

Andy had already selected the spot to anchor Sheik. Two cottonwoods in the grove had grown to massive proportions with only three or four feet separating them. The sturdy chestnut mare, used to planting her feet and staying while her rider worked with recalcitrant steers, proved invaluable in getting Sheik into the proper position. Andy quickly crosstied the stallion between the trees, wisely leaving him blindfolded and hobbled. Tomorrow would be time enough for removing the bandanna. "Okay, old boy, let her rip." Andy slackened and removed the rope that bound Sheik to Chinquapin.

Sheik exploded as much as a horse so bound could do. He neighed and screamed, lunged and fought. The crosstied ropes from the hackamore to the cottonwoods on either side of him obviously infuriated him. So did his hobbled feet. By the time weakness from his ordeal stopped the performance, the stallion stood hot and sweating.

Andy automatically reached for the tin pan to give him water. He stopped and slowly shook his head. Cruel as it seemed to let a horse go hungry and thirsty, if he ever meant to tame the black, he must deprive him of food and drink for a day or two. Nothing else could make Sheik amenable to even the most loving, tender care. He eyed the drooping horse standing exhausted. For a single moment, Andy hated himself. Why should he imprison this animal, any more than he'd clip the wings of a high-soaring eagle? Yet, if he did not, someone else would.

"I guess I'll love you more than anyone else could," he told Sheik. Chinquapin perked her ears, and he hastily added, "Not more than you, Pard. You're the best." The chestnut rubbed her soft nose against his shoulder, then ambled over to stand near the tied stallion, far enough away that if he lunged, she'd be out of striking distance, close enough so her soft whinny reached him.

Andy noticed how the drooping ears lifted and the way Sheik raised his head. An answering whicker confirmed the cowboy's suspicions. If he tamed Sheik, a lot of the credit must be given to his faithful Chinquapin.

All through the night, he heard the restless stirrings of the captured stallion. Andy slept fitfully, yawned himself awake at first light, and built a fire. Hot coffee, bacon, and biscuits from the night before, toasted over the coals, sent new energy through him, although he could barely tear his gaze free from Sheik. Just before he'd opened his eyes, Andy had felt it all a dream. It seemed impossible the black stood securely tied just yards away.

"Sheik, I hate keeping you like this," he told the proud and unbeaten horse who lunged toward the sound of the voice. The crossties held firm, and Andy darted in, snatched off the bandanna blindfold, and leaped back, none too soon. Instead of appreciating the slight freedom, Sheik plunged and tried to rear, acting more enraged than ever.

"At least it tells me you aren't hurt too badly." Relief washed over the slim cowboy. Morning light reflected small gold twinkles in his laughing brown eyes, and his corn-colored hair tossed wilder than ever. "Sorry to do it, but you'll have to go without feed another day. Once some of the ginger gets out of you, we can get on with the business of turning you into a grand saddle horse." He also left the rope hobbles on. Ahead lay the need to check the gashes on Sheik's flanks to make sure they healed without infection, and wicked, flying hooves didn't lend themselves to doctoring.

Bright sun poured into the hidden valley. Sheik settled into an uneasy doze broken by periods of fighting the ropes. Andy took pity on him in late afternoon, snubbed him to Chinquapin's saddle, and let the veteran cow pony lead the black into the creek. He again poured icy water over the stallion's back and sides and grunted with pleasure when he saw how nicely the wounds were coming in the healing air. This time when Andy crosstied Sheik, he left a tiny bit of slack in the ropes, just enough so the horse could lower his head and drink the small amount of water his new master placed in the pan.

"No use trying to get you to drink from my hat," he told the stallion. "Right now you're hating the man smell most as much as you hated the slide. If you behave, tomorrow you can eat."

By the next evening, a vastly subdued horse stood between the cottonwoods. All day he had eyed his herd, grazing in the thick green grass Andy withheld by keeping the crossties tight enough to prevent Sheik's mouth from reaching the ground. He had stayed quiet most of the day, especially when Chinquapin devotedly hovered nearby. Andy noticed how the big black alternated between ignoring his captor and stealing glances at him. He whistled and saw Sheik's ears prick. "Old boy, someday you'll come when I whistle," he promised. "Same as Chinq does." He affectionately pulled the mare's mane, and she rubbed her nose against his shoulder. "With you as stud, maybe I'll get me a little spread back near the Double J, raise horses, and get married."

His eyes opened wider. Not since his early infatuation for Columbine Ames had he dreamed of ever settling down. A slow smile crawled over his expressive face. A boy's shy admiration had been successfully diverted from lovesickness to a staunch friendship. Not a pang smote Andy when he saw Columbine and Smokey Travis stand and take wedding vows. Neither had Andy's frank approval of the girl from Payson he once thought about courting amounted to anything serious. Heart whole, he had ridden away with no regrets.

"Funny, me thinking about getting hitched," he told the quiet valley. Yet in spite of his preoccupation and thrill of the conquest, his anticipation of the days, perhaps weeks he would need to break Sheik, the vision of a snug cabin with a couple of kids playing near its door and Sheik, Chinquapin, and their colt or filly close by, persisted in knocking at his heart's door.

CHAPTER 3

At the same time Andy Cullen restlessly waited for winter to pass so he could go wild horse hunting, storms beat New England with a vengeance. Linnet Allen, as small and birdlike as the finch for which she had been named, disconsolately stared into a snow-swirled January afternoon from a conveniently placed velveteen settee. Usually she loved the view from her Boston home. Seasons came and went with the same regularity that ruled the eighteen-year-old girl's life with her father.

From the highly polished window glass, a shadowy figure distorted by the snow into a caricature of the brown-haired girl with the soft blue eyes stared back at her. Pale skin gleamed and made her thin face all planes and angles. She raised a frail hand to blot out the sight, then deliberately blew on the chilled glass. A mist rose, obscuring her image. Before it could vanish as her girlhood dreams had done, she traced her name, then the date in the beaded moisture. *Linnet Allen, January 17, 1892.* She stared at the word. If what she felt in her heart came to pass, she wouldn't be there to write the date in 1893.

No tears fell at the thought as they had the first time she realized how weak she'd grown. From childhood, Linnet had been taught the plan of salvation. She had no fear of dying. Her mother already waited in heaven to welcome the beloved daughter she'd left behind years before. Without morbidness, Linnet considered her situation, and when the mist came, she knew that pity for the father who adored his only child inspired her tears.

She hastily brushed them away. For as long as God allowed her to remain, she must play the game with her father, pretending that one day she'd be well and strong. Even when his brown hair whitened and his blue eyes so like hers wore sadness, they continued pretending for each other's sake. Sometimes she wondered if he thought she didn't know how short a time she had left and kept up the game to spare her. Words often trembled on her lips. How much better to bring things into the open! Yet each time, she stilled them. Perhaps her father found comfort in believing she had a future. If so, Linnet must not take it away from him.

Such long years of invalidism, ever since her mother died. Linnet counted them on her fingers. She'd just been seven years old when her mother died giving birth to Judson George Allen, the baby brother who lived only long enough to open his eyes for a single look at the world before following his mother. Eleven years, yet so clearly imprinted on her memory that Linnet recalled each detail with astounding clarity.

"Linnet, Darling, Mother and Baby Judd have gone to live in heaven with Jesus," her father told her, his voice muffled against the little girl's soft hair.

She sat stock-still, unable to comprehend. *"But Mother said I'd have a little brother or sister."*

"You do, but he had to go with Mother."

"Does God need them more than we do?"

The grown-up Linnet still flinched at the memory of her father gathering her close and brokenly saying, *"Perhaps. We still have each other, and someday we'll see Mother and little Judd again."*

The despondency didn't come all at once. A sharp bout with influenza left Linnet weak and subject to grief. Judd Allen did everything possible to help. He called in

45

specialists who examined her, shook their heads, and mumbled platitudes. One forward-thinking doctor declared that the loss of a mother and the baby brother she'd been promised, combined with the high fevers from her illness, had left an indelible mark. In time, Linnet recovered enough to be up and about but with only enough stamina for limited activities. A heart specialist said the muscles of her heart evidently had been weakened and that she must rest and not extend herself.

Linnet docilely followed orders. She ate and drank what the servants brought her, dabbled in the kitchen when she felt like it, and lived life through the wealth of books her father provided. Her keen mind far outstripped her frail body. A succession of governesses and tutors helped her to develop her mental faculties. She not only devoured the classics and romantic novels but avidly read newspapers and delighted her father with her perceptive insight into current problems. By her sixteenth birthday, Linnet Allen had earned the reputation of possessing wisdom beyond her years. She had also made such splendid physical progress, that her father proudly talked of sending her to college.

How her blue eyes glistened! For the first

time in her life, she'd be normal, live with other young women her own age, study and make friends, perhaps even fall in love. Pale rose swept into her white skin at the thought. The most beautiful love story she had ever heard came from her own parents. Would God someday send a man as strong and caring as her father to share her life?

A week after her birthday, her rosy illusions shattered. A sudden fluttering of her heart, followed by sharp pains, served notice that the strenuous college life she coveted must forever remain out of reach. A conclave of physicians agreed on that completely.

"Darling, I know how disappointed you are," her father gently told her. His face looked careworn in the dim light of a dying fire. "There's a good side, though. I won't have to be here all alone."

Linnet summoned all her courage, smiled, and gaily told him, "That's right. I'll be here to make sure you take care of yourself."

The attack ended as suddenly as it had come, with no noticeable aftereffects. Still, a change had entered the Allen household. A deepening of the pretend game; an acceptance on Linnet's part of her uncertain life span. If sometimes she rebelled, she reminded herself that God loved her and knew best. Her deepest pain lay in concern for the father who would have no one except God. The depths of his faith would see him through, but how many lonely years would he face before joining his family in a world without tears and sickness and parting?

A heavy step in the hall, quicker than usual, and Judd Allen entered the quiet room. "What? Sitting in the dark?"

"I hadn't noticed," Linnet truthfully said. "I've been watching the storm." She smiled and rejoiced at the look of gladness that replaced the anxious expression he wore when feeling unobserved. A white envelope dangled from his well-shaped hand. "A letter? From whom?"

"Your uncle George."

Excitement lent color to her pale face. "Really?" Uncle George rivaled Sirs Lancelot and Galahad in Linnet's list of earthly heroes. A year younger than his brother Judd, the breezy, tanned man swept into the staid Boston home like a sturdy western breeze on his infrequent visits. He looked ten years younger than Judd, with his sun and laugh wrinkles around the Allen blue eyes. Linnet's greatest dream had centered around growing well enough to one day visit her uncle's Rocking A ranch in far-off Utah.

Judd Allen turned up the gaslight, and the shadows fled from the big room to hover waiting in the corners. Linnet ignored them. Lips parted, she leaned forward.

"Here, little finch, you read it." Her father tossed the letter into her lap.

With eager hands, she tore open the envelope and read the bold scrawled words aloud.

"Dear Judd and Linnet,

I find I won't be able to get back East for a visit this spring or summer after all. Seems like it's getting harder all the time to get good, reliable hands. The sheriff relieved me of three of my newest not long ago on account of their taking ways — taking critters that don't belong to them.

Why don't you hop on the train and come see me? The Rocking A's the best place on earth to get some meat on your bones, Linnet. You can ride and walk and sleep with windows wide open to the fresh air. Best thing in the world for you. You, too, Judd. Last time I saw you, you looked like city death. Come on out here, and we'll fatten you on prime beef-steak.

George

P.S. Better yet, how'd you like to buy

half of the Rocking A? Sell home and business, and come live with me. The ranch house is big enough for a dozen. We'll marry Linnet off to one of our Utah or Arizona cowboys and fill the house with their kids. This lonely old bachelor's hankering for kinfolk and someone to carry on the ranch after he's gone."

A peal of laughter came from Linnet's lips at the prospect. Every picture of cowboys and ranches, all Uncle George's stories of the real West with bawling cattle and ornery horses, cliffs and floods and canyons, melded into a colorful, beckoning life that lured with its mystery. The unknown as well as the known tantalized Linnet.

"How I'd love to go!" Her thin face glowed with excitement. "Father, could we?"

The lines in Judd Allen's face deepened as if drawn with heavy black ink. "Darling, I don't see how."

She read the unspoken reason in his face. In her condition, she'd be lucky to get out of Boston before collapsing. Disgust with herself for not fighting mingled with sharp longing. "If I get better, can we go?" She hated the pain in his eyes and bit her lip. Yet rebellion churned inside. She would die soon. She knew and accepted it. Yet must she die before she had ever really lived? Before she saw anything other than Boston and the nearby shore? *Never!*

The little word her heart shouted made her gasp. She willed her body to relax. The one thing the physicians agreed on was her need for peace and quiet. On the other hand, what had they given her except a lassitude that robbed her of the will to walk more than a few steps?

Linnet jerked back from her thoughts when her father lifted one of her pale hands and jokingly asked, "Think these could hold the reins? Or is it that cowboy husband George promised that makes you so eager to go west?"

She tried to match his mood. "Maybe." She forced a grin. "Wonder if Uncle George thinks any cowboy will do or if he has one in mind?"

"I hope not!" Genuine alarm rang in her father's voice. "Think how disappointed the bowlegged specimen would be if he's expecting a bride from Boston and you should arrive, fasten that blue gaze of yours on another cowpoke, then leave Bowlegs dangling!"

What a sport he was. Linnet pretended to

wipe her eyes free of laughter to hide the mist. "You haven't answered my question," she accused. "Besides, not all cowboys are bowlegged, are they?"

"I don't know," he admitted. His eyes darkened. "If you get well enough to go by spring or summer, I'll take you." He hunched his shoulders, stood with legs apart and hands on his hips. "We'll fork a coupla hawses an' ride off into the sunset, right, Pardner?"

Her proper Bostonian father looked so ridiculous, Linnet couldn't help laughing again. "Sooo, you've been reading Western novels instead of business reports, have you?"

He haughtily raised his head and looked down his nose at her. "My dear daughter, do try to control your vulgar curiosity. Any well-informed man attempts to become familiar with a wide variety of cultures —"

"Including the American West?" she teased.

"Of course." He looked embarrassed, and his eyes twinkled. "I have to confess, I've always envied George and his life on his ranch."

"Really?" Linnet sat bolt upright. Never before had her father indicated in any way dissatisfaction with his lifestyle. Had he secretly longed to break free of their long line of proper ancestors as Uncle George had done when young? Had she held him back with her invalidism? She winced at the thought. The seed of an idea sprang into her fertile mind. She started to speak, then snapped her mouth shut. This wasn't the time. First she must consider and pray.

"Would you ever think over selling out here and going in with Uncle George as a partner?" She tried to make the question insignificant and felt she'd failed miserably but saw that her father found nothing abnormal in it.

"Depends on what time of day or year it is," he said. He patted his lean stomach, "Speaking of time, isn't it nearly time for dinner? I'd better wash up." He strode to her, leaned over, and dropped a light kiss on her forehead.

Linnet noticed the new spring in his step and felt it answered her question more fully than his words did. Uncle George's letter had raised her father's spirits, no doubt about it. The trickle of knowledge fell on the planted seed and watered it.

The entire dinner table conversation centered around the Rocking A, Uncle George, and his remarkable letter.

"I think he's lonely," Linnet frankly stated while the maid removed the remains of the main course before serving dessert.

"One of the things about remaining un-married is the lack of someone to grow old with," her father replied. "I know that's poor grammar, but it's true. Another thing. The more years one accumulates, the more important family grows unless there are bad feelings between family members."

"You really miss him, don't you?" Linnet put down the silver spoon she had picked up to use with her fluffy pudding.

"Yes." The simple word held a world of longing.

For the first time, she saw him not as her father but as a man with whom life had not always dealt kindly. Strong, faithful to the God of his forefathers, he kept the com-mandments learned at his mother's knee and had successfully battled adversity without allowing bitterness to creep in. Yet all these years he must have missed the wife he'd adored and the little son given for such a brief moment. Linnet knew he had poured out all his love to her, never seeming to need other companionship. The warmth of her awareness centered on her rapidly sprouting idea, and by the time she went to bed in her four-poster with the lovely counterpane, that idea had become a bud, then a full-blooming flower.

Wide awake long after she normally slept, Linnet considered every aspect of Uncle George's letter and tried to arrange the petals of her idea in a logical order.

"First, God," she prayed, "Father and I have to speak frankly. Playing our pretend game won't work any longer." She dreaded the confrontation, but it loomed large and was a formidable foe to her rapidly burgeoning plan. Until they faced her health situation honestly and together, nothing else could happen.

"Next, what does it matter if I die here or in Utah? I know You're with me. If I can only grow strong enough for the train journey, it will get Father away from Boston and all his sad memories. He will have that someone to grow old with that he spoke of when discussing Uncle George." A feeling of rightness crept into her heart.

"God, I can't tell him I want to do this for him, or he won't let me take the risk. I have to convince him it's my last wish, and if he takes me west, he's fulfilling it." She sighed in the darkness. Fooling her father wouldn't be easy. Yet, was it really fooling? She *did* long to see something other than the pictures from her window and the sights of Boston in the carriage rides growing less and less frequent, due to her declining health.

"Dear heavenly Father," she prayed just before sleep claimed her. "All of this can only happen if it's Your will, not what I want or think is best." She turned over and knew no more until a light tap on her door announced morning.

"Breakfast in bed, Miss Linnet?" the maid asked as she poked her head through the doorway.

Linnet thought of her new resolve. "No. I'll slip on a housecoat and slippers and come down." She smiled at the maid. "Thank you for lighting my fire. You slipped in so quietly, I never heard you."

"My pleasure, Miss." A flash of friendship passed between the two, one so sturdy and useful, the other, frail and hampered. "Can I help?"

"No, thank you. Just tell Father I'll be down, please."

"Very good."

The door closed. Linnet slid from beneath her covers, quickly washed her face and hands in the bowl of steaming water that greeted her every morning, and donned a warm wrapper and slippers. "Uncle George never said what conveniences his ranch house has. Wonder if I'll have to wash in ice water and build my own fires?" She shivered at the thought. "Well, God, here goes." She slowly made her way downstairs to the pleasant breakfast room.

Judd Allen's blue eyes shone when she came in. He left his position in front of the roaring fire in the fireplace and led her to the nearby table hopefully set for two. The storm had stopped, and pale winter sunlight gleamed through the windows and sparkled off glasses and silver. "How are you this morning, little finch?"

"Hungry." She didn't tell him her long hours of scheming had taken extra energy and left her famished. "What do we have for breakfast, hot biscuits and beefsteak?" She tipped her head in a pert manner.

Judd Allen burst out laughing. "Whoa, young lady. You're confusing this with the Rocking A. I'm afraid you'll have to settle for porridge and muffins or scrambled eggs, bacon, and fruit."

"A buttered muffin, then eggs, bacon, and a glass of milk."

His eyebrows shot up. "I thought you hated milk."

"Milk comes from cows. Cows live on the Rocking A," she told him. "Therefore, I will learn to like milk. Even if I have to hold my nose when I drink it. Milk is good for me," she droned in an imitation of a pompous physician who had thrown up his hands when she said she never drank milk.

Judd stared at her. All trace of mirth left his face. "Linnet, you know this is just pretend, don't you? We can't go to Utah."

His grave manner set her heart fluttering. "Let's talk about it after breakfast, Father." She smiled, and her lips quivered. She steadied them when he nodded, then managed to choke down a creditable breakfast.

Once the breakfast things had been taken away and the maid had shut the door, father and daughter settled into matching chairs across from each other in front of the blazing fire. Its cheery crackle mingled with the sunlight streaming in and added brightness to the small, pleasant room.

Linnet plunged in, taking only a moment for a final, silent prayer for guidance. She leaned forward, laced her fingers together on the soft blue flannel of her housecoat, and began, "We've needed to really talk for a long time, Father."

He didn't pretend to misunderstand. "I know," he said heavily. Despair, along with grief, settled into his face.

"I'm eighteen years old. Before long, I . . . I'll be gone." In spite of her best efforts, her voice broke.

"Linnet, if this is too hard for you, let it go." Judd Allen left his chair to kneel beside hers and take her frail hands in his strong ones.

She shook her head. "No." She looked at him, beseeching him to understand. "It's just that . . . I can't die when I haven't really lived." Words tumbled out, a dictionary of them, spilled by necessity into the quiet room and the ears of a father who loved her second only to their heavenly Father. She told him how she longed to go west, to see the fields and plains, the prairies and rivers, and mountains in between.

"You know the chance you'd be taking?" he hoarsely broke in at one point as his hands tightened on hers.

"I know. I could die on the way, except somehow, I don't think God will let that happen." Assurance she hadn't realized filled her lent credence to her prediction.

"Even if you could reach the Rocking A, all those things George promised are impossible. The riding and —"

"Bowlegs," she finished. A ripple of laughter shook her, but she found her eyes strangely wet. How foolish to weep over a cowboy she had never even met! "It doesn't matter. At least I'll have had that much."

"Don't you want to be, I mean . . ." He couldn't go on.

It took her a few seconds to comprehend. She freed one hand and patted the kneeling figure's brown hair. "I'll be with Mother and little Judd. They won't care about anything else. I think they'd also like my grave to be where you could visit it." She sensed he'd reached the breaking point. "Father, why don't we go? As soon as spring comes? You can do as Uncle George suggested. Sell out here, and plan to stay out west." She played her trump card. "You could keep him from being lonely." *And he will do the same for you,* she knew.

With an inarticulate cry, Judd released her hand and caught her close in his arms.

Linnet's heart leaped. She hadn't won yet, but she would. She must. In no other way could she ensure happiness for the man who meant more to her than anyone else in the world.

CHAPTER 4

The first discussion began a new era in the Allen household; other long talks followed. In the new atmosphere of honesty with pretense put aside forever, Linnet and her father grew closer than ever. She sometimes felt herself leaving girlhood behind and taking on the maturity of a young woman. She also saw how clearly she had been willing to continue as the pampered, loved child instead of accepting responsibility as a partner, thereby relieving her father of some of the load they now carried on a more equal basis.

Their former adult-to-child relationship changed as well to an adult-to-adult sharing that permitted both of them to open their hearts as never before. Linnet learned the depths of the love that her father still held for her mother. Many times tears secretly sparkled on her lashes. She would never love or be loved in that way. The shadowy image of the man who might have been her husband sometimes haunted her. She could never conjure up a face but smiled when he always wore a wide-brimmed western hat like her uncle George's Stetson. Although it had been several years since Uncle George had visited Boston, Linnet's mind remembered every detail of face and costume, especially the Stetson.

January snowed itself into February. February pouted and dallied between winter and early spring, much like a Southern belle at a cotillion flits from suitor to suitor. Linnet paid little attention. She embarked on a get-better program of her own creation. It included drinking milk and even learning to tolerate it, although her father teased and said the Rocking A ran beef cattle, not dairy cows. She slipped into soft, noiseless slippers behind her closed bedroom door and paced back and forth until her heart twinges reminded her not to overdo it. By the first of March, she had actually gained five pounds and could walk twice as long as before. She didn't tell her father. Raising false hopes would be cruel, yet Linnet couldn't help but know that the results of her hard work gradually began to show. She smiled, comparing her determination with the spirit of her ancestors that long ago fired them to flee religious persecution and settle in the New World a few crossings after the *Mayflower.*

Not until time for her next physician's visit did Linnet allow herself to hope too much. The surprise in his face and his, "Well, Miss Linnet, looks like you're holding your own, at the very least," brought joy to the household. She made a face at the spring tonic he prescribed to "help you continue as you're doing" but obediently swallowed it.

Linnet also secretly opened her bedroom window to the cold air and took great breaths into her lungs, knowing the physician would throw up his hands in disgust at such a practice. She'd read that a new school of thought believed fresh air to be beneficial rather than harmful. It made sense. If God didn't want people to breathe His air, He wouldn't have created it, she firmly told herself.

One evening in late March, Linnet marched downstairs and into the dining room. "Father, I need new clothing. I can barely fit into my old clothes."

"That's the best news you could give me," he told her. His eyes shone. "What kind do you need, eastern or western?"

She impulsively hugged him and felt

excitement race through her. "What about simple garments I can wear in both places? May will be a nice time to travel, don't you think?"

"Let's make that in June. Less chance of snow in the high mountains that way." He courteously seated her at the table and sat down across from her.

"You mean we are really, truly going?" Linnet had trouble believing her own ears.

"I promised I'd take you if or when you were able to make the trip, didn't I?" His face wore the biggest smile in the world. It slowly faded when he added, "I have a good offer on the business. Shall I take it? By the way," he added in an offhand manner that didn't fool Linnet one bit, "the buyer of the store also likes this house."

She felt his questioning gaze on her. For a moment, she hesitated, feeling torn between the secure but unsatisfying life she'd known here and the uncertainty of life in the West. A terrible fear smote her. What if she were running before the Lord, arranging her life and her father's on a girlish whim to meet the selfish desire for adventure that dwelled within her? She risked a quick glance at her father. It vanquished fear. He looked even younger than Uncle George on his last visit. Some of the strain had gone from his face.

Longing rested in his blue eyes, and eagerness showed in the way he held his knife and fork still, waiting for her reply.

"When do we leave?" she asked.

"I suggest June fifteenth."

Odd how the setting of an actual date made the venture real. Linnet felt a smile blossom onto her lips. "That should give me time to get a suitable wardrobe ready and to sort and pack what we want to take with us." She cast an affectionate look at some of the old, highly polished furniture. "Will Uncle George have room for it?"

"He said the ranch house is big; we'll have to ask how big."

One by one, things settled themselves into place. Linnet and her father thanked God when the new owners of the house and store eagerly agreed to keep the Allen servants on. None of them evidenced any desire to go west. "Too Boston," Judd announced. A frown wrinkled his broad forehead. "Can you get along without a maid on the train?"

"I can and will." Linnet stood straight and proud. "I'm so much better now, she wouldn't have anything to do."

April passed; May came in a cloud of blossoms. Eager as she was to leave, Linnet had to admit that the Boston spring had never been lovelier. Or perhaps it came with the fact that she now spent much more time outdoors, walking as well as riding in a carriage. A slight cold near the end of May, combined with drizzly weather, dampened their spirits. Surely after selling out and making such careful plans, Linnet's heart wouldn't flare up now. She shivered more at the thought than from her cold and laughed off her father's suggestion that they postpone their journey. Even when she didn't regain energy to the point she had been before the cold, she refused to consider waiting. A feeling of urgency drove her.

"How much strength does it take to sit in a train and look out the window?" she demanded when her father showed concern. "I'm just glad we have the money for first-class accommodations. Ever since George Pullman came out with his Palace Car Company's sleeping cars, transcontinental travel has been a lot more comfortable, at least according to the papers."

"You're right about that." Judd looked amused. "I've seen them. Burnished walnut fittings, heavy damask draperies, and deep plush seats that convert to beds are a real boon. I'd never consider taking you if it meant going coach. The poor folks who ride in them sleep where and as best they can, jammed together in sometimes dirty cars on a first-come, first-served basis."

That night Linnet dreamed of railroad cars. She saw herself running through endless cars filled with a wider segment of humanity than she'd ever seen before: cowhands and schoolteachers; dirtily clad miners traveling to new diggings; farmers and drummers with their wares. Some ragged, some bearded, some wearing revolvers. Now and then a professional cardsharp who gathered his victims in the parlor car and set about fleecing them. Still she ran, searching for she knew not what, until sharp pangs in her heart slowed her feet to a standstill.

She awakened hot and sweaty, tangled in her bedclothes. It hurt to breathe. Fear set her heart pounding. "God, are You here?" she whispered. Gradually her pulse quieted, and her breathing returned to normal. Yet the memory of the dream and its aftermath lived on. At first sign of light, she rose, reached for her Bible, and turned pages, hoping for a talisman to which she could cling. She knew God stayed near at all times. Yet if only she could find a special verse, one she could make her own letter from God along with the Twenty-third Psalm, John 14:1–4, and of course, John

3:16. Twenty minutes later she found it. Psalm 27:14: "Wait on the Lord: be of good courage, and he shall strengthen thine heart: wait, I say, on the Lord." She flipped a page of her well-worn Bible and discovered the same thought phrased a little differently in Psalm 31:24. "Be of good courage, and he shall strengthen your heart, all ye that hope in the Lord."

Comfort flowed through her like an incoming ocean tide. She slipped back into bed, still holding the Bible. "God, I don't know if this promises actual healing, but it says You will strengthen my heart if I wait and have courage. I already have the blessed hope You give through Your Son. Please, help me accept whatever Your will is in my life. In Jesus' Name. Amen."

Soothed, she fell asleep again and awakened to a new day, a new opportunity to wait and hope and practice that "good courage" of which David spoke.

In response to a hearty invitation to "ship any and all of your goods to the Rocking A," the Boston home had been depleted of favorite pieces of furniture. Trunks of her mother's dishes, protected by handmade quilts, had gone ahead, and most of the Allens' belongings would be at the ranch to welcome them. Linnet had patiently stood while a skilled dressmaker took her new measurements and later came back with new gowns, a riding skirt, and waists, undergarments, and petticoats to be tried on and admired. A heavy dark blue traveling costume hung waiting and ready in the closet, along with a matching hat. The private car they reserved meant Linnet and her father would be able to bathe and change clothing whenever they wished.

"And you'll wish real often," the droll railway ticket agent warned. "Even the Pullmans aren't immune from dust."

Linnet decided on the spot to wear the dark blue with several changes of waists on the trip west. "No use getting everything filthy," she announced. "I'll change when we go in the dining car for meals, though."

"You'll be the prettiest young woman there." Judd Allen's pride in his daughter oozed from every pore and brought a rich blush to her normally pale face, which had rounded out a bit under her get-better regime.

The time before leaving dwindled to a few weeks, a week, days. Any time Linnet felt weary, she repeated "her" psalm, took fresh courage, and thanked God for allowing her to make the trip and get her father settled with his brother on the Rocking A. Beyond that, she refused to think. Should, by some miracle, her life continue in Utah, it would bring great joy. For now, she found it enough that they could go.

Of all Linnet's new clothes, she liked her riding outfit best. She pushed from her mind that she might never wear it astride a horse. The dressmaker had cleverly fashioned the divided skirt so that when Linnet stood straight, she appeared to be wearing a full skirt that covered the tops of the boots her father had specially ordered. Nothing could be more modest or more convenient. "Unless I wore boys' pants." Linnet giggled and twirled to show how much freedom the divided skirt gave her. The rich dark green skirt had a pretty vest to match, with a creamy long-sleeved blouse and a clever green cap her father said would blow away in the first wind.

"Then I'll get a sombrero or Stetson," she bragged. "I wish I could wear these clothes all the time instead of my gowns that require —" She broke off and blushed again. Nice girls didn't discuss corsets with their fathers. She had wisely refused to let the dressmaker sew one of the new hourglass styles that demanded tight lacings to make her waist as small as possible. She had tried on such a dress, one ordered and rejected by another customer. She couldn't breathe well and heaved a sigh of relief when she got out of it.

Now she giggled again. The dressmaker had confided from a mouth filled with pins, "Miss Allen, I hear the girls and women in the West don't wear corsets at all. Can you believe that?" She pursed her thin lips.

"Maybe they're too busy being abducted and carried away on racing horses to worry about it," Linnet had said.

"No *lady* would go without a corset, regardless of the circumstances." The woman's look of horror quelled Linnet but didn't keep her from muttering under her breath, "Well, this lady is *not* going to be squeezed to death for the sake of fashion! I can't wait to wear my riding clothes. No one will ever know if I have on a corset or not."

The thought delighted her until she wondered why she hadn't realized how much she rebelled against what "they" say. Perhaps "they" would stay in Boston and she'd be rid of them and what they said when she got out west.

The only hard moment in all their leaving came with the final visit to the cemetery. Judd Allen and his daughter stood by the simple headstones that commemorated wife

71

and mother, son and brother. Hands clasped, each offered a short prayer that they would be true to the God who made them and one day be reunited with Him and the rest of the family. When they turned away, Linnet felt the way she did at the end of a book, even though she knew a sequel was beginning. She looked at her father and, as happened so often, knew he understood.

An ending, a beginning. Then what? How long would Linnet's life last? *"He shall strengthen thine heart."* Her often-repeated verse ran through her mind. She closed her eyes, heart overflowing. Then she silently followed her father to the carriage that would transport them to the railway station. *Good-bye, Boston, with your snow and blossoms, your security and sameness. Good-bye, cemetery, home once happy that became a prison. Good-bye, good memories and sad. I'll take you with me,* she promised.

The carriage rumbled its way over the streets. Judd Allen said nothing. Linnet clutched his hand the way she'd done as a child. Once they left the city, they could relax and look forward. Now was the time to reflect and remember. Somehow, she knew without being told that neither she nor her father would pass through these familiar streets again. A few tears fell, and she surreptitiously wiped them away, knowing she wept for what might have been had Mother and little Judd lived, not for the long years in between.

America unrolled before Linnet and Judd Allen's fascinated gazes like red velvet carpeting before visiting royalty. Each state added its unique terrain to the great tapestry that made up the land of their birth. Accustomed to Boston and Boston alone, the travelers frankly gaped at stretching fields, hills and valleys, countless rivers, and uninhabited miles. The steady *clackety clack* of the wheels sang them to sleep, and they rolled relentlessly onward. The stopover in Chicago felt endless, and Linnet breathed a sigh of relief when they again took up their journey. Still, she admired the way the city's residents had pitched in and rebuilt their city after the terrible October 1871 fire.

"Did the fire really start in Mrs. O'Leary's barn?" she asked a fellow traveler who sat at the next table in the luxurious dining car.

"Oh, yes. It's a matter of history. A cow kicked over a lighted lantern," the helpful man told her. "The summer of 1871 was exceptionally dry, and in the evening of October eighth, strong winds sent flames racing north and east. They leaped the river

73

and killed at least three hundred people, plus doing two hundred million dollars in property damage. My family and I were among the fortunate." A look of remembrance crept into his eyes. "We shivered in the lake for what felt like hours." He shrugged off unpleasant memories. "But so many fine architects seized the chance to help rebuild, that in less than fifteen years, Chicago became the nation's architectural capital," he finished proudly.

Linnet tucked the information away, as she did whenever she learned new things. All that damage, started by a single cow! Just like sin, starting from a seemingly innocent event, then fanning into a conflagration that destroys everything in its path. Her quick mind made a further connection. Those who escaped the devastating results had taken refuge in the lake. God offered refuge, too, through His Son. Those who came to Him need have no fear of the raging world behind them.

The look of the land changed. Linnet rose each morning and tantalized herself by not flinging apart the rich draperies that curtained her berth and not looking out the window until she had washed and dressed. Every day proved worth the self-discipline. Rolling hills gave way to flatland; farms and cornfields to grasslands. A small herd of buffalo grazed not far from the railroad tracks, and Linnet clapped her hands in delight. Her father's expression told her the sight thrilled him just as much as it did her.

Yet nothing could compare with their first glimpse of the Rocky Mountains. "I used to think the pictures artists painted had to be larger than life," Linnet confessed, face pressed to the window. "No picture can ever do this justice." Jagged peaks serrated the blue sky. Fat white clouds rested for a moment on the tops before scooting away to join their mates. Gigantic evergreen trees stood in sentinel ranks.

"Semper fidelis," Judd softly quoted. "Always faithful."

Linnet could barely tear her gaze away from the scenery long enough to eat. From a full heart, she whispered, "Father, no matter what happens, this trip is right. I've worshiped God since childhood but have never felt His power and greatness so much as right now. It's like having a Best Friend for years and suddenly growing aware of how much more than a Friend He really is."

Her father's sympathetic silence and quick squeeze of her hand showed how deeply her words moved him.

The one bitter drop in the smooth amber honey of their journey west occurred the day before they reached Salt Lake City, where they would leave the train. Through visiting with friendly, congenial people in the diner, they'd heard many of the exciting stories of early railway travel and of how blizzards and spring floods played havoc from late fall to early spring. They rejoiced at their decision to wait. June had been lovely, and outside of a few blinding rainstorms and one thunder and lightning episode that left the Easterners wide-eyed, sunny days prevailed. Neither had they encountered ruffians, as some of the old-timers riding the train said used to barge into the palace cars. "Cowboys thought it fun to do some shooting and see folks duck," one leathery man told them. "Desperadoes held up trains, too, and took money and jewelry. We haven't had any of that for a spell."

"Don't speak too quickly," another bronzed outdoorsman put in. "We aren't there yet."

Linnet's overactive imagination proved her undoing. Sheltered by the damask draperies, she lay awake and nervous. "Don't be a silly goose," she admonished herself. "The man said these things didn't happen now."

Yet she uneasily shifted position. What if a marauder burst in and demanded jewelry? Father had advised her to wear none on the train, but a fine string of pearls lay tucked in the toe of a slipper in her traveling bag, and Father's luggage held a small jewel case with a few other choice pieces that had been Mother's. Linnet had kept the pearls close, wearing them only in the privacy of their accommodations and putting them away at night.

Now fear assailed her. Wouldn't robbers look in the bags first of all if they came? The longer she lay there, the more upset she grew. Perhaps she should get up and move the pearls. She could pin them inside her high-necked, long-sleeved nightgown. She quietly sat up so she wouldn't disturb her father and, with one hand, reached to open her berth's draperies. A slight sound turned her to ice. Linnet held her breath and noiselessly slid the draperies open just enough to peer out. Suddenly, she felt faint. In the dim light cast by a one-eyed moon, a dark figure knelt on the floor not more than two feet from where she lay.

CHAPTER 5

For the space of a heartbeat, Linnet stared at the crouching figure before the words of her psalm rang in her brain. *"Be of good courage."* Anger she hadn't known she possessed raged through her. How dare this creature creep in here to plunder and rob decent people? She sprang from the bunk. "Who are you, and what are you doing?" she demanded.

"Linnet, Darling." The figure straightened.

"Father?" She reeled and clutched the side of the berth for support, keeping her voice low. Relief sagged her knees to the consistency of the pudding served at dinner.

"My head ached, and I thought you might have something in your bag. I didn't mean to frighten you." Remorse filled his voice.

"It's all right." She sat down on her berth and pulled her feet up from the richly carpeted floor. "I guess I just heard too many stories of intruders." She stifled a giggle. "There are some tablets in the small box." She lay back down, conscious that her father had found the tablets and had gone back to his berth. Yet the incident had taken its toll. A faint twinge in her chest reminded her that all the travel in the world, all the majestic mountains and cool, green valleys didn't change the unalterable truth. Linnet sighed and whispered, "God, I bargained with You for enough strength to get me here for Father's sake . . . and mine. Now I'm not content at all. Oh, but I long to ride and run and be free! Must I wait until I reach heaven to do all these things?" More forlorn than she had been in months, she closed her eyes, and for the last time, the clacking wheels sang her to sleep.

Uncle George had arranged to meet them in Salt Lake City. "No stagecoach for you," he had written. "I'll be there with the prettiest pair of high steppers you ever saw and a buggy I designed specially for good riding. It's a long ways to the Rocking A from Salt Lake, and we'll take it in easy jaunts. Linnet, wait 'til you sleep with nothing except space between you and our Utah stars."

He was true to his word. Linnet stepped down from the train and into her uncle's waiting arms. He looked even bigger and browner than she remembered him. "Well, Lass, you're here." His keen gaze made Linnet feel he could see clear to her soul.

"Yes." No other words came. She wanted to pinch herself to make sure she wouldn't waken and find herself still in Boston.

George turned to his brother. He slapped him on the back, then gripped Judd's hand with a mighty paw. "Welcome, Pardner."

"Just remember, you're speaking to the new half owner of the Rocking A," Judd told him. His eyes flashed, and Linnet saw how much alike the two were. Except for the gray in her father's hair and his whiter skin, they could be taken for twins. Again, the sense of rightness about their journey warmed her through and through.

"What do you think of the West?" George asked them when they'd stowed away their traveling bags. "Uh, Linnet, don't you want to get out of those clothes and into something, well, a little more rugged? You, too, Judd."

Linnet looked down at her travel-worn outfit. Even the linen duster she'd worn for protection hadn't kept the dust off. "I hate putting on my pretty new riding outfit," she confessed to her uncle.

"You don't have to." George looked sheepish, then produced a large package. "I

80

wasn't sure you'd have the right clothes so I brought some." He undid the string. "These should fit." He held out a heavy shirt, jacket, and jeans to Judd. "They're mine."

"And whose are these?" Linnet bit her lip to keep from laughing when he handed her a matching outfit, only smaller.

"We keep extra clothes on hand in case some ragamuffin cowpoke rides in," George said easily. He took a violently patterned red kerchief from the bottom of the parcel, then an equally bright blue one. "Tie these 'round your neck under your shirt collars. They help stave off dust and sunburn. There's a couple of sombreros in the contraption."

Linnet took the blue kerchief and eyed the curiously constructed buggy. Two-seated, it stood waiting on four high wheels.

"For fording streams," her uncle explained. He pulled a pocket watch out. "I hate to hurry you, but —"

"It's a long way to the Rocking A," Judd and Linnet chorused before repairing to the ladies' and gentlemen's rest rooms to change into western garb.

When Linnet stepped back outside, she felt more self-conscious than ever in her life. She looked totally unlike herself. The dark blue jeans fit as if tailored for her; so did

81

the dark blue shirt. She'd tried on the sheep-lined jacket and knew how comfortable it would be once night fell. Neckerchief tied in a jaunty knot, she practically skipped to the contraption. Uncle George stood talking with a stranger, who turned out to be her father, looking as unfamiliar in his new clothes as she felt.

"Glad you chose the blue scarf," her uncle approved. "It matches your blue eyes." He helped her into the surprisingly soft backseat of the buggy, waited until Judd climbed into the front seat, and clucked to the matched pair of bays. "Giddyap there, David, Goliath." They moved off in perfect unison.

"Why do you call them that?" Linnet wanted to know.

Her uncle grinned back over his strong shoulder. "David in the Bible obeyed God. So does the horse on my right."

"And Goliath?"

"He's inclined to be lazy. He'd go lieth down if David didn't keep him moving."

Linnet started at her father's shout of laughter and the way he slapped his knee. She couldn't help joining in, and she thanked God for the sound. In all their years since her mother and little Judd died, she'd never heard her father laugh like that.

Tears actually came to his eyes before he could stop.

"You never did say how you like it out here," George reminded, hands steady on the reins of the trotting pair.

Linnet found herself stammering. "It's big and kind of scary and awe inspiring and . . . and I love it all."

"Good. Now we'll show you some real country."

"I thought that's what we'd been seeing," Judd protested.

"Wait until you see the red-rock canyons and the valleys so green you wonder how the good Lord could make them that way." George's voice lowered. "Or purple and flame sunsets and sunrises, nights darker than black velvet 'til the moon comes out and lights up the world."

He drove on in silence so deep that his guests refrained from questioning him. "It's a grand country, this Utah Territory. One of these days we're going to be a state and the best one in the Union." He warmed to his subject. "It's got everything a man — or woman," he glanced back at Linnet again, "everything anyone could want. A lot of hardworking people have come and put down roots both here and in Arizona Territory, folks like me and now you."

Linnet's heart pounded as he talked. How much she had missed, confined to her velveteen settee, even though the changing seasons from her window offered beauty. It contrasted sharply with the land they traveled toward Moab, this ever-beckoning, protean land of stunted trees, small hills, mesas, rearing mountains, purple-shadowed forests in the distance. "Uncle George, tell me about the ranch."

He remained silent so long that she wondered if he had heard her. Then he quietly said, "Lass, I can tell you everything there is about the ranch and you still won't know it, any more than the folks who know all about Jesus but don't have the smattering of an idea what He's really like. You have to walk and ride the land, sleep out, get caught in storms and by early nightfall. Then you'll know the Rocking A."

"She can't do all those things," Judd reminded in a low voice. His shoulders slumped, and some of his joy left his face.

"Maybe not now. Give this wonderful land a chance. Time and again, I've seen folks come out here to die, then they find themselves made well by the air and peace our Father put here." He broke off, then added, "Of course, there's a lot of hazards. Mean broncs — we won't make you ride them right away — rattlesnakes, and not all of them crawl on their bellies." A thread of steel undergirded his warning. "Worst thing won't be a problem to you, Judd, just to Linnet. Lovesick cowboys aren't worth their feed."

She felt a blush start at the base of her throat and crawl under the blue kerchief and into her face. She couldn't resist demurely asking, "We wondered, when your letter came, if you had a special cowboy in mind for me."

"Naw. And believe me, any hand who thinks he's going to up and run off with my niece is facing two Rocking A owners to please. Right, Judd?"

"Right."

George abruptly changed the subject. "Would one of you like to drive?"

"I . . . I'd better not," Linnet faltered, even though her hands itched to get on the reins. A new and disturbing personality had been donned with her new garb, one who longed to forget heart problems and drink her fill of this strange life.

"I'd love to, if you think it's safe." Judd's glance toward his brother spoke volumes to the young woman watching from the backseat.

"David and Goliath will do what you tell

them. Whoa, boys." George reined them in and changed seats so that Judd could easily reach the brake if necessary.

Linnet marveled at how quickly her businessman father had shed eastern reserve. Within moments, he handled the team as capably as his brother and won a covert glance of admiration followed by a canyon-sized grin from George.

Conversation subsided. Linnet realized for the first time how tired she had grown. Excitement had kept her going on the long train trip. Now she felt she could sleep for a month in the pungent, sagebrush-scented air that occasionally held a whiff of clover. She turned sideways, curled up on the comfortable seat, and relaxed, first her body, then her racing mind. She slept, roused to the men's low voices, then slept again. Once she wondered if she'd be the only woman at the ranch. Would she make friends in Moab, the nearest town? She sleepily smiled. Running in on neighbors or to a store out here meant a major undertaking, unlike Boston and its multitude of houses and shopping establishments. She yawned, too tired to pursue the thought.

"Should we wake her?" Her father's question brought Linnet back to consciousness. "She won't want to miss anything."

She started to open her eyes and stopped when George's reassuring, "She won't. These few red rocks are nothing compared with what's ahead. Let her sleep," reached her.

Linnet lay in a cocoon of peace until George said, "Now's a good time to tell me everything. How bad is she?"

She wanted to cry at her father's sad answer. "The doctors say it's just a matter of time. Her heart's been weak for years, and I've had her to every physician I could find."

"Including the Great Physician?"

"Always." Linnet had to strain to hear her father's confession. "I've never been able, at least yet, to tell Him that if it's His will to take her, it's all right with me."

The eavesdropping girl surreptitiously slid a hand over her mouth to keep from exclaiming. Poor Father. Her heart ached for him.

"You will, when the time is right." George's heavy hand fell on his brother's shoulder. "Now, let me make sure I understand. As far as you're concerned, it will take a miracle to save Linnet."

"Yes."

"Will you let me try? I'm no doctor, but if it isn't going to make a difference, I'd like to give it my best."

"What do you propose?"

Linnet lay like one dead. Every nerve end tingled. What amazing suggestions would this hero-uncle have other than the usual orders to rest, take her medicine, and so on?

"Throw away her corsets, first of all."

The subject of discussion found it nearly impossible for her to keep from howling. If the dressmaker could hear Uncle George! Linnet could imagine her face.

He wasn't through. "Judd, it doesn't make sense that women can squeeze themselves into instruments of torture until they can barely breathe and not do harm to their innards. How can a heart be healthy and do its job without plenty of room to beat?"

Linnet wanted to applaud. He'd merely echoed the new sentiments she'd recognized during her final dress fittings.

"She adores you. I think she'll do as you ask," Judd mumbled. "What else?"

"Exercise. Walking every day. Naturally her heart's weak when she hasn't done anything to strengthen it. My finest stallion and filly would soon become useless if not properly worked out."

If he hadn't been dead serious, Linnet's control would have broken. *First, no corsets;*

second, compared with a fine horse. What next?

"Have her walk until she starts to feel tired, then not one minute more. My Indian friends have a recipe for living that the white man would do well to adopt. 'Eat before you get hungry; rest before you get tired.' In other words, don't wait until you're starved or exhausted, then try to make up for it by stuffing yourself or sleeping long hours. How's her appetite?"

"Better since we planned to come out here."

George grunted approval. "It'll improve when she exercises. No dainty meals for her, either, but good, honest grub that will build her up. I'm a pretty good hand at cooking, although I've always eaten most of the time in the cookhouse or had a Chinese house-boy. When I found out you were coming, I hired the best cook in the territory. Name's Mrs. Salt, and can she cook? I should smile, she can. Salt by name and salt of the earth, as the old saying goes. She'll mother Linnet to death, of course. Lost her own family years ago in a stagecoach accident. Since then she's been head cook in a Moab boardinghouse, but I offered her twice the wages plus a job as long as she wants it."

"What's she like?"

"About our age." George laughed heartily, and Linnet quickly closed her eyes when he glanced her way before lowering his voice. "If I wasn't a confirmed bachelor, I'd marry her. She's a dandy. Looks like one of those helpless little ladies who can't keep their parasol from blowing away but works like a mule. The ranch house hasn't been this clean since I had it built."

"Does she have a first name?"

"Sure, Sarah. Just don't call her by it. When I talked to her about taking on the Rocking A, she looked at me and said, 'I'll be happy to come, Mr. Allen, and I'll expect to be treated as a lady. That means being called Mrs. Salt.' Well, I'd eaten her flapjacks and apple pie, and I wouldn't have cared if she wanted to be called Queen Victoria. I assured her she'd be well treated, and next thing I knew, she packed her stuff and took over the Rocking A," he ruefully finished.

It also finished Linnet's self-discipline. She burst into laughter.

George quizzically looked back at her. "And just how long have you been awake?" he inquired.

"Long enough to hear all about Mrs. Salt," she told him between giggles. When they subsided, she added, "I actually heard all about your plans for me."

"Do you agree?" His piercing gaze again went to the core of her being.

"With all my heart," she fervently agreed. She saw her father's hands relax a bit where they had tightened on the reins. "I'll be as obedient as David, even if you tell me to go lieth down when I don't feel tired." She felt rewarded for her sally when her uncle bent a mock stern look toward her and shook his head, although his lips twitched. It encouraged her so much, she plaintively said, "It's too late to eat before I get hungry. I'm starving right now."

"Good." His warm look of approval preceded directions for Judd to turn off the road just around the next bend. In the shade of a clump of cottonwoods near a barely moving stream, Linnet watched her uncle uncover a white-wrapped basket and spread the cloth on the leaf-strewn ground. Fried chicken, tiny biscuits, jelly, even chocolate cake followed. Water from canteens provided a drink.

"Manna in the wilderness." Linnet bit into a perfectly cooked chicken breast after her father thanked God for bringing them this far and for the food. "Compliments of Mrs. Salt?"

"No. I had it packed in Salt Lake." George smiled at his pretty niece. "It's good but not as good as my new housekeeper-cook's."

An incredible amount of food later, Linnet stretched, then prepared to curl up for a few moments of rest. Instead, she discovered her uncle had already started to carry out his plans for her when he ordered her to walk.

"You'll have plenty of time to rest in the carriage," he kindly told her. "It's —"

"I know. A long way to the Rocking A."

George's eyebrows rose, but his eyes twinkled. "Has she always been this sassy?" he asked his brother.

"No. It must be in the air," Judd teased.

They traveled until late afternoon. George and Judd spelled off driving the team while Linnet dozed or watched the changing country. It had grown rougher, with steep hills that made even the strong team slow down far before they reached the top and increased their pace down the other side. Rusty-looking dirt had replaced the gray and yellowish soil. Jackrabbits and cottontails bounded through the sage, paused to examine the carriage and its occupants, then went on with their lives. Linnet exclaimed a hundred times at their antics and at the many birds she saw. The only things she hated were the greedy black birds of prey that her uncle called buzzards. "Ugh, they're so ugly." She jerked her unwilling gaze from two of them feasting at the side of the road.

"They're necessary," George said briefly. "They clean up remains of animals that die."

Still, Linnet felt glad when the carriage rolled past and she could no longer see them.

Uncle George didn't allow Linnet to help with camp preparations. "Walk," he told her. "But don't go far. You never know what might be lurking 'round here."

She instantly peopled the quiet spot with a horde of desperate bank robbers, rustlers, and wild animals bent on destruction, then laughed at her fancies. *What a tenderfoot I am! Why can't I be more like Father?* She watched him interestedly while she strolled back and forth in the circle of light cast by the snapping fire that he had helped Uncle George build. One observation and her father duplicated his brother's actions, even taking over and mixing the biscuit dough while Uncle George laughed and watched him. He also helped remove the soft seats from the carriage to make beds.

"What about you, Uncle George?" Linnet asked after the men spread blankets and prepared two couches as easily as the porters on the train whisked seats into berths.

"I'm used to the ground." He threw down a tarpaulin, a couple of blankets, and checked the biscuits baking in a pan he called a Dutch oven. He examined the strips of mouthwatering bacon sizzling on sharpened sticks propped close to the fire, then opened a can of peaches. "Supper's ready."

Linnet couldn't believe how many biscuits she stowed away, along with bacon strips and a large helping of peaches. Under the protection of the carriage top, she changed into her nightclothes. She left her comfortable garb lying smooth for the next day, then slipped into her bed.

"After you've been out here awhile, you'll sleep in your clothes," her uncle George predicted.

"Maybe." She stared at the stars, white against a purplish-black sky. The one-eyed moon she'd seen from her train window had opened its eye a little more and added a sheen to the camp. The fire sputtered and died. A distant owl hooted. Linnet Allen pulled her blankets closer around her and slept.

CHAPTER 6

Long before the Allens reached the Rocking A, the eastern members of the family were wholeheartedly, unreservedly in love. The wild country that had long since claimed George in his younger days now wove invisible, silken threads of possession about Judd and Linnet. Southeastern Utah's red buttes and cliffs, its arches and twisted formations, held the visitors spellbound — as did the blue-and-purple-shadowed canyons that yawned at their feet.

"Wait until you see Dead Horse Canyon," George promised. "In spite of its gruesome name, it's one of the grandest spots in the state."

"What an odd thing to call a canyon!" Linnet's soft blue eyes opened wide.

Her uncle repeated the same legends that Andy Cullen had overheard in the Moab cafe weeks earlier. He finished by saying, "That trip will have to wait until you're stronger. A man might get a wagon in drawn by mules, but the contraption isn't built for it."

Discouragement dimmed Linnet's anticipation, and she quickly covered a small sigh. Not for anything would she confess how tired the trip had left her. In spite of good food and fresh air in addition to many naps, even the spectacular scenery had begun to pall. She sometimes felt that if she could only get to the Rocking A and sink into a bed, nothing else would matter.

Did Uncle George sense her feelings? Perhaps. In any event, he casually announced, "We can either go clear home tonight or camp out once more."

Judd Allen anxiously looked at his daughter. "Linnet, it's up to you."

"I would like a hot bath," she admitted. "I seem to have accumulated a lot of . . . trail dust, didn't you call it?"

"Home it is." He whistled cheerily and clucked to the team. At the word "home," David and Goliath pricked their ears and stepped out as briskly as if they hadn't already pulled the contraption many miles that day.

Linnet relaxed on her comfortable backseat and let the country flow past until the combination of relief and late afternoon

June sun lulled her to sleep.

She awakened to darkness, the whinny of horses, and yellow light streaming into the contraption from a lamp held high.

"Bring her right in, poor thing. She's tuckered out, I reckon," a woman's voice ordered.

Still half asleep, Linnet felt strong arms lift and carry her up shallow steps, across a wide porch, and into a house brightened by lamplight and the flames in an enormous open fireplace. The crisp, kindly voice went on giving directions, and the tired young woman wanted to bury her face in her uncle's shirt and cry. She caught a glimpse of a blue-and-white-checked housedress covered with a huge, spotless white apron but didn't look into Mrs. Salt's face until her uncle gently set her on her feet. Brown hair lightly touched with gray framed a face that showed lines of sorrow but great strength. Compassionate blue eyes as keen as her uncle's peered deep into Linnet's thoughts.

"Run along, Mr. Allen. This young woman needs a bath and bed."

The ghost of a smile trembled on the weary traveler's lips when he meekly replied, "Yes, Mrs. Salt," then beat a hasty retreat. She remembered Uncle George saying that the housekeeper-cook had taken over the Rocking A when she arrived.

"Mercy, Child, you're all bones and no meat," the motherly woman scolded, hands busy divesting Linnet of jacket, shirt, and jeans. She threw a wrapper over the slim, white-clad girl and led her to a nearby bathroom complete with a large tub filled with warm water. "Here's your soap and washcloth and towels. Do you need any help?"

"No." She smiled at Mrs. Salt, who stood perhaps an inch shorter than Linnet's five feet, five inches and outweighed her by about ten pounds. "You are so kind."

"Now, holler if you need me. I'll just warm a gown for you and have it ready when you are." She stepped into the hall and closed the bathroom door behind her.

Linnet wearily let the wrapper slip to the floor and got out of her chemise and long cotton drawers. The warm water and sweet-smelling soap washed away both grime and the terrible, all-gone feeling that had attacked her in the final homestretch. Still tired but feeling better, she washed her hair, soaped it again, then poured clean water over it from a pitcher Mrs. Salt had thoughtfully placed nearby. Then she wrapped herself in a bedsheet-sized towel.

"I'm ready, Mrs. Salt."

The little woman with the big influence bustled in, handed her a fire-warmed nightgown, and considerately turned her head so Linnet could slip into its folds. "Come sit by the fire," she invited, and the new Rocking A resident obediently followed her to a small, padded rocker.

Refreshed by her bath, Linnet took notice of her surroundings, something she hadn't done when she first arrived. "A fireplace in my own room. How nice."

"There's one in each bedroom plus the big one in the living room," Mrs. Salt told her.

"And, why, this is my rocker." Her gaze sped around the room. "And my bed and dressing table."

Mrs. Salt chuckled and vigorously rubbed Linnet's wet hair. "The boys had quite a time of it, hauling your furniture here and getting it set up before you came. Not that they weren't glad to do it," she added smugly. "I just showed them that picture of you that Mr. Allen has on his desk, and you never saw such a hurrying around to offer their services." She took Linnet's comb and brush from the dressing table, and the young woman realized that Mrs. Salt must have unpacked the train bag.

With long, smooth strokes, the woman gently worked out tangles until the brown hair curled just above the toweled shoulders. "We'll turn your back to the fire," she said. "That hair needs to be dry before you go to bed. It's pretty hair. Do you always wear it short?"

Linnet nodded. "The doctors said long hair tired my head, and Father likes the short curls. I feel it makes me look childish, but it's easy to care for."

"Sensible, that's what it is," Mrs. Salt approved. "How do you like your room? We tried to make it as much like yours in Boston as we could but had to depend on Mr. Allen's memory of it, and he isn't much for noticing specifics."

"It's beautiful but different. A nice different. I didn't have hand-braided rugs on my floor or whitewashed log walls, but I like them. They're homey."

"Good. Now I'll bring you some supper, then I have to get the men fed. Mr. Allen will be hungry."

"So am I," Linnet admitted. "I eat a lot more since I left Boston, although I forced myself to eat there when I knew we might come west." She sat perfectly still, content to let the snapping fire do its work.

"In a few weeks, we'll get you built up so

you aren't just a remnant, weak and small."

"A *what?*" Linnet roused from the stupor induced by the warm water and fire and stared.

Mrs. Salt raised her eyebrows and looked innocent. "You know, in the song 'All Hail the Power of Jesus' Name.' You're a Christian, aren't you?"

"Yes, but —"

To Linnet's utter astonishment, the amazing housekeeper-cook sang in her rich voice:

"Ye chosen seed of Israel's race,
Ye remnant weak and small,
Hail Him who saves you by His grace,
And crown Him Lord of all."

She ended by saying, "Child, we're glad you came," then she trotted out.

Linnet laughed until the tears came. A "remnant weak and small." Perfect description for a frail person as well as the faithful who followed the Lord. She tipped her head back to capture more of the fire's warmth. God had often taken just a remnant of believers and done mighty things. He could have chosen twelve hundred disciples to carry on His work. Instead, He'd selected twelve — physically strong, many of them, yet subject to spiritual weaknesses. Who

101

knew His ways? She yawned, and Mrs. Salt's entrance with venison stew, hot corn bread, homemade applesauce, and an extra large glass of milk roused her only long enough to eat before tumbling into bed. Mrs. Salt tucked her in the way she'd do a child and swooped down to place a soft kiss on the white forehead.

"Sleep well, Child. God is watching."

Again the urge to cry came, but Linnet successfully fought and overcame it. She would not be a baby, even though this was the first woman's kiss she had received since her mother died.

Dreamless sleep did what no amount of bathing or good food could. She awakened feeling rested and a little indignant when Mrs. Salt, her father, and Uncle George agreed that a day in bed wouldn't hurt. She had so much to see in her new home. Why, she hadn't even examined the house in which she would live, or the corral or outbuildings or the scenery that lay outside.

"You have the rest of your life to explore," Uncle George told her. His blue eyes like Father's showed how clearly he knew her inner rebellion. "There's just one thing. . . ."

She looked at him inquiringly.

"Lass, everyone here loves you and will

do what they can to help. I know you'll co-operate." Not a trace of a smile creased his bronzed face. "Above and beyond all that, your health and life is in the Lord's hands. I'm not a magician or a miracle worker. Neither is your father or Mrs. Salt. We're going to treat you according to plain old common sense, but God will have the last say. If you get well and strong the way we hope, it's because that's His will."

"I know." She took both of his calloused hands in her slim, white ones. "I'll do what you say." A wistful note crept into her voice. "Would it be all right if I lie on a couch instead of the bed? I . . . I'd like to be with you all."

Mrs. Salt wiped her eyes on her apron and took command. "No reason at all she can't rest on that pretty velveteen settee the boys hauled down from Salt Lake. It's by the window in the living room, where she can see what's going on outside as well as into the kitchen where I'm working. Child, can those white fingers of yours do needle-work?"

Linnet glanced at them, and red shame crept into her face. "Why, yes. I've embroi-dered and crocheted and —"

"Ever done any plain hand sewing?"

Her head proudly came up. "I have."

"Good. I've a bundle of flannel that needs finishing into little garments. A family in Moab lost their home in a fire, and they need all the help they can get. I haven't had time to do more than cut them out and pin the seams. If you feel like it, it would help out a lot."

Linnet caught the way Uncle George's mouth opened and felt he planned to protest. Mrs. Salt sent him a quelling look, and he subsided. The same rueful smile that Linnet had seen him wear a few times before returned, and he gruffly said, "Whatever Mrs. Salt says is all right with me."

"Thank you, Mr. Allen." The bland response couldn't quite hide her satisfaction.

Judd Allen hovered over his daughter once she'd been established in the comfortable living room with its sparkling windows, white ruffled curtains, Boston furniture mingled with brightly colored Indian blankets, and more hand-braided rugs on the polished board floor. Finally, she caught his longing look out the window and told him, "Go find Uncle George and get to work. We can't have one owner of the Rocking A do all the work around here, can we?" His face lit up like a child seeing his first pony, and the sound of the big front door closing behind him showed his eagerness to begin his new life's work.

Linnet also started working on the soft flannel clothes for the unfortunate children. Between kitchen duties, Mrs. Salt drifted in and out, once to bring a glass of milk and warm molasses cookies from a recipe she said had been in her family for generations, another time just to see how the sewing was coming. Linnet proudly held up a finished garment and felt an inordinate sense of pride at the good woman's praise. She also discerned exactly what Uncle George had meant about his housekeeper-cook. She never raised her voice or seemed hurried. Yet a luncheon that Uncle George called dinner appeared on the table at twelve o'clock sharp; an equally appealing supper was ready at six o'clock. And each meal had appeared after a deceptively small amount of effort that hid a mountain of work.

By the third day, Linnet felt she knew Mrs. Salt well enough to ask, "Now that we're here, what are you going to call Uncle George and Father? They can't both be Mr. Allen."

"I'll think on it."

Linnet had a feeling she'd hear those words a million times in her acquaintanceship with the motherly woman. They typified the caution inherent in Mrs. Salt of wanting to make wise decisions. Finally, the housekeeper-cook said, "My employer will remain Mr. Allen. If your father doesn't mind, I will call him Mr. Judd."

Both men readily agreed, but Linnet saw how quickly they averted their gaze and suspected how much they wanted to laugh.

Mrs. Salt had a teasing side, as well as her efficient one. Her blue eyes twinkled on a rare occasion when she considered her household duties caught up enough for her to sit with the new daughter of the house and sew. "Didn't I see Reddy Hode and Tommy Blake come in here a little while ago?"

"Yes. They wanted to know where Uncle George had gone. I guess he forgot to give them orders for the day," the unsuspecting Linnet told her. "Charlie Moore came, too."

"Those scalawags. They know perfectly well where they're supposed to be and what they're to do." Mrs. Salt laughed, then frowned. "I suppose it's to be expected. Even rough cowhands like to be around pretty young women, or I should say, especially cowhands. I'll have a word with Mr. Allen."

"Please, don't," Linnet said in alarm. Her heartbeat quickened. "They seem like such nice boys, I wouldn't want them to get into trouble." She shuddered at the thought of being the unwitting cause of young men losing their jobs.

"They're nice enough, I'll hand them that. Not like some we've had." A look of forbearance rested on her face before mirth replaced it. "I'll wager we won't have trouble getting and keeping riders now that you're here. Reddy and Tommy and Charlie won't be the only ones stricken with memory loss that sends them up here to the ranch house . . . not with you sitting there, so dainty and pretty."

"It is pretty, isn't it?" Linnet lifted a fold of her pale yellow gown that looked like a drift of sunlight in the room.

"Yes."

Linnet had a feeling that Mrs. Salt didn't mean the gown. The time since she reached the Rocking A had removed nervous strain from her body and painted a faint pink in the cheeks beginning to round out from good food and the twice daily walk Uncle George insisted she take. True to her word, she stopped the minute she felt tired. Yet each succeeding day found her able to walk a little more without her heart fluttering. She had been introduced to the cowboys, who awkwardly removed their big hats and nudged each other bashfully when she offered her white hand to be swallowed up in their brown paws. She'd seen a parade of horses and longed for the strength to ride. She faithfully thanked God for her progress and refused to look ahead more than a day at a time.

Now, all the talk around the ranch concerned the Independence Day doings in Moab and whether Linnet should go. Naturally, the cowboys loudly proclaimed it wouldn't hurt her a mite. Uncle George and her father reserved judgment, making no decision until Mrs. Salt advised that she didn't see any harm, so long as Linnet took it easy.

On the night of the third, the excited girl had a hard time falling asleep. Visions of bucking horses, expert riding, flags, and fun swirled in her mind. Would all the cowboys be as nice as Reddy, Tommy, Charlie, and the other Rocking A hands? They evidenced none of the uncouthness that many Bostonians associated with their kind, and she knew, without being told, that any one of them would fight to the death to protect her or her good name.

Being placed on a pedestal had troubled her until the frank Mrs. Salt said, "Child, it's good for them to have someone to admire and hold high. Who knows? The way you live your life as a witness for the Lord may be making a far deeper impression on some of our boys than any of us know."

After that, Linnet put aside false embarrassment and simply treated them all the same. Showing favoritism could be disastrous, according to her wise mentor and friend who to some extent had stepped into a mother role.

The mighty Colorado River proved to be disappointing. Due to the hot summer, its wide banks held more red hard-baked clay than sluggish water. "It's a mighty different thing in flood," Mrs. Salt told Linnet from her position next to her in the backseat of the contraption. She pointed out marks showing how high the river had risen, and Linnet gasped, finding it hard to believe the innocuous-looking water could reach that high.

Moab more than made up for seeing the Colorado River's low level. The long main street swarmed with people like ants to a picnic; bright holiday clothing rivaled the red-rock canyons and walls that Linnet never tired of seeing. Indians in buckskin, heavily fringed and beaded, stood aloof, arms crossed.

"Wait until you see them ride." George

Allen's eyes glistened. "Some of them have wonderful horses, right off the range. You can't get a finer horse." The corners of his mouth turned down. "I should know. My best Arabian mare was stolen by a wild stallion. I'd give a gold mine to get her back along with the colt sired by the stallion."

Linnet was too intent on the story to blush over the discussion. She'd learned that westerners found nothing objectionable in talking about life and birth among the animals. "Who owns the colt?" she asked.

"Good question. I suppose since his mother's mine, I could make a claim, but first I'd have to catch him." George haw-hawed. "Besides, in this country, a wild horse is considered to belong to the man with grit enough to capture and tame him." He grinned down at the niece who clung to his and her father's arms. "By the way, the boys have Sadie gentled and ready. Soon as we get home from this shindig, we'll try you out on her."

Linnet thought of the white mare who took sugar and carrots from her hand. A thrill went through her. "I can hardly wait!"

"Maybe we should just load up some supplies and head for home," her father teased, looking more than ever like his brother. "What's an Independence Day celebration compared with riding Sadie?"

His daughter squelched him with a reproving, "Father, really," but her laughter spilled over. "It's so good just to be here and be part of all this." Her glance took in everything from the general store to the livery stable. She watched an old man walk from the stable and noticed his keen gaze beneath shaggy brows, the same quality that characterized Uncle George and Mrs. Salt.

"Mrs. Salt, we need more thread," Linnet remembered.

The housekeeper-cook paused in her task of unloading from the contraption a dinner basket, cloth, and a blanket on which to sit. "Run along to the store, Child. Do you need money?"

"Just put it on my bill," Uncle George told her. "I'll be in to settle up later."

Laughing and flushed with the unusual events, Linnet picked her way through the still-growing crowd toward the general store. She held up the skirt of her yellow dress to keep it from dragging in the dust and tried to keep from being jostled by the good-natured throng, wondering if a fish swimming upstream felt this way — pressed and harried. She finally reached her goal, and a surge of humanity swept by. Linnet glanced over her shoulder to wave to Mrs.

Salt. She didn't notice that someone had come out of the general store until it was too late. Carried forward by her determination to get the thread quickly so she wouldn't miss anything, she ran full tilt into a solid body.

"Whoa, Miss." Two strong arms shot out and respectfully but firmly kept her from falling.

Linnet felt a warm blush color her face. Annoyance at her carelessness snapped her head back. She looked up, straight into the brownest eyes she had ever seen, sparkling with laughter and the slowly dawning look of one who had waited for this moment a long, long time.

CHAPTER 7

"Is this yahoo bothering you, Miss Allen?" one of the ranch hands asked. The supporting arms fell from her shoulders, and Linnet glanced over at Reddy Hode, his hands on his hips in a protective gesture. Tommy Blake and Charlie Moore flanked him like twin avenging angels. Where had they come from, she had time to wonder before the stranger spoke.

"Sorry, boys. She plumb ran into me, and I had to grab her so she wouldn't fall."

"Is that right?" Reddy assumed his usual role of spokesman for the trio and sounded suspicious.

Linnet's sense of humor saved the situation. "If I'd been walking any faster, I'd have knocked him clear back into the store." Her merry laugh rang out even above the din in the street, and her self-appointed guardians relaxed.

Reddy generously held out his hand to her

rescuer. "No offense, Mister. We didn't see her fall. Just saw you grabbing at her." Tommy and Charlie murmured assent.

The cowboy, who topped Linnet's height by perhaps four inches, smiled until his eyes crinkled under the shock of ripe corn hair that sprang into unruliness when he courteously doffed his Stetson. He gripped Reddy's hand, then Tommy's and Charlie's. "I don't blame you a bit. If I'd seen you doing the same, I might have bulldogged you first and asked questions later." His joyous laugh robbed the words of their sting, and the Rocking A hands and Linnet joined in.

"Linnet, haven't you got that thread yet? It's almost time for —" George Allen stopped short and glared at the four cowboys surrounding his niece. "What's going on here?"

"It's all right. I'll tell you later." Linnet urged him into the store. "I almost fell, and that cowboy caught me."

More laughter bubbled inside her like a mountain spring. "I don't know him from Adam, except by now, I suppose Adam would have an awfully long beard if he were still around."

"Oh, the joy of having a pretty niece!" He rolled his eyes. "Get your thread, Lass, before you start a riot."

The Rocking A hands took pains to inform her they'd never seen the stranger before but that they saw him riding out of Moab on one of the prettiest chestnut mares in the country. "Called her Chinquapin," the loquacious Reddy added. "Don't know why he didn't enter her in the race. She looks strong and fast."

Linnet hid her disappointment. In the need to get Uncle George away before he made a scene, she hadn't even thanked the cowboy! Her cheeks felt scorched and not from the weather, hot as it had grown. He must think her stupid and ill-mannered. She couldn't even write a note. No one appeared to know him or anything about him except that he rode a chestnut mare called Chinquapin. She sighed. If he were just passing through, a little splinter of regret would prick her all the rest of her life.

An urchin clad in nothing visible except a pair of bibbed overalls raced toward them. "Didja hear? Didja hear the news?" He ran out of breath.

"What news?"

"There's a myst'ry horse gonna be in the race." He ran on to tell anyone who cared to listen.

"Mystery horse?" Linnet repeated. Not Chinquapin, surely.

Her uncle's tolerant grin settled her down. "Every year someone enters some so-called mystery horse. Usually it's a joke . . . a nag who can barely make it to the starting line." He stopped, raised to the toes of his boots, and stared over the crowd. "Jumping jackrabbits, look at that horse!" He audibly swallowed. "It's the spitting image of —"

The roar of the crowd drowned him out. Linnet clutched her father's arm and tried to see. Why should a horse, even a mystery horse, send such a look to Uncle George's face? For a second, the crowd swayed. She peered through the crowd, and her heart bounced. Not at the proud black stallion prancing down the street but at the rider, whose corn-colored hair fell over his forehead and partly hid laughing brown eyes.

Andy Cullen had dreamed of this moment since the first time he heard that a black stallion named Sheik roamed the ranges with his band. Now the noise and color faded. In the space of a few moments, the long weeks in the hidden valley returned. He had broken many horses in his years on the range but none like Sheik. He reveled in the magnificent black's spirit and determined to use patience and love rather than the harsh methods fellow horse breakers employed that resulted in a dispirited, cowed horse.

Lack of food but sufficient water aided Andy in his task. He gradually loosened the crossties between the two large cottonwoods enough so that Sheik could eat the grass his new owner pulled and the precious handfuls of oats. It took time for the stallion to reconcile himself to Andy as the source of his food and the tin pan of water noisily slurped. He also grew accustomed to being led snubbed to the faithful Chinquapin's saddle.

Late spring warmed into early summer. Bees droned and staggered drunkenly from an abundance of wildflowers. The valley lay undisturbed except for the band of horses who curiously eyed the goings-on of their lord and master. Time and again, they crowded close but kept a respectful distance from Sheik's lunges against the ropes.

The beautiful June day that Andy first got a saddle on his captive went down in his memory as one never to be forgotten. He'd already tamed Sheik to a point where he unwillingly accepted the feeling of a saddle blanket. The heavy saddle, though, brought out all the fight that made the black horse the king of the range. He kicked up a storm and continued it until he stood dripping wet and exhausted.

"Good boy!" Andy shouted at the top of his lungs. "You'll get used to it. Maybe I'll turn you into a race horse and sell you for enough to buy that spread I want." Yet, even as he said the words, he knew the impossibility of selling Sheik. A pang went through him at the thought of anyone else even riding Sheik, let alone owning him.

Day by day, Andy won Sheik's trust. The stallion suffered the man's touch, although he trembled. Andy instinctively felt the time had come for his first ride. Left toe in the stirrup, he vaulted to the saddle. "Yippee-ay!"

Sheik went into every contortion known to bucking horses, then added a few choice ones of his own. Jolted, hair soaked from sweat, face fiery, Andy hung on for dear life, keeping the black's head up and back. *If he ever got it between his knees, look out, Mama!* What felt like an eternity later, the expert rider gave Sheik just enough slack to stretch out and run. "We're riding the wind, Boy," Andy yelled. Up the hidden canyon they pelted. The horse herd ran for their lives, away from their charging master. Only Chinquapin dared follow, but even her strength and speed could not come close to Sheik's. A wide turn. Back down the valley floor. Up. Back. Andy wondered who would tire first, he or the horse. Just when he knew he could endure little more, the stallion slowed from a dead run to a gallop, then a trot, and at last, a walk. Spent, Sheik stood shaking while Andy rubbed him down. A slap on the rump sent him to his waiting band, Chinquapin still at his heels.

Every day, Andy mounted Chinquapin, cut Sheik from the herd, then lassoed and saddled him. He discovered that the stallion hated the landslide area and maneuvered him in that direction when he could. Every day, Sheik went through the same bone-crunching performance until Andy despaired of ever mastering him.

June waned, and July loomed close. The wild horse hunter lost track of the date. He continued to work with Sheik and one day reaped rich rewards. Sheik had long since learned to prick up his ears at Andy's whistle. On a day that dawned so beautiful it made the cowboy's insides ache, Sheik answered the morning whistle, raced to him, then pranced away like the show-off he had become. His few pitches once Andy mounted were clearly halfhearted, and he settled into the fast rush up and down the canyon that his rider suspected he'd come to love.

"You're broken, you're grand, and you're mine," Andy exulted. He reined in the stallion and rubbed his neck. "Good thing, too. I've been out of flour for two days, and the rabbits are getting scarce. What say we go get some supplies, old boy?"

Sheik whinnied and shook his head before looking toward his band of followers.

"What are we going to do with them?" Andy scratched his head in dismay. "All these weeks, how come I ain't considered your family, old boy?"

Sheik whinnied again.

"Maybe I'd better just leave them here for the time being," Andy mused. "There's plenty of water and grass. The landslide that almost made a dead horse out of you blocked the exit to this hideout of yours. If I roll a few boulders into the trail behind us when we go out the way I tracked you in, they'll be fine."

Chinquapin pressed close to her master, rubbed her soft nose on his shoulder, and looked at him with intelligent, soft eyes that reproached him for transferring allegiance to the stallion.

"Not you, Chinq. Sheik's used to being led tied to your saddle." Yet Andy scratched his head doubtfully. Leading a rope-hobbled Sheik in the confines of the canyon was a far different story than expecting the black to suffer such indignity on the open range, and a lot of miles lay between them and Moab.

"I just can't leave you here, Sheik. What if someone happened on you? Now that you're broken, would you let another cowpoke ride you?" He thought some more and decided the only way out lay in riding Sheik and letting Chinquapin follow. The mare's love affair had progressed at an amazing rate. Andy hoped she'd never have to choose between following Sheik or her owner.

His plan worked beautifully. He filled canteens with water for their journey and picked his way out of the valley leading Sheik and letting Chinq follow down the narrow trail. Once outside the crowding walls, he tied the horses and walked back to the spot where the trail widened into the valley. "Can't let any of the other horses get into the narrow passage and find it blocked at the other end," he reasoned. "They wouldn't be able to turn." Grunting and tugging, he rolled boulders into a rough barricade high enough to discourage a horse from attempting to climb over.

"Wonder what that sharp-eyed old man at the livery stable's going to think when he sees you?" Andy asked his new possession.

Every time he thought about riding down the main street of Moab, his funny bone tickled.

"If those four galoots who think they're going to drive you out on Dead Horse Point and fence you in are in town, they'll get the surprise of their lives," he told Sheik. A moment later, Andy's smile of anticipation died. He had caught and tamed the stallion, but the black wore no brand. Horse thieves abounded in southeastern Utah, and Sheik would cause even an honest horse lover's eyes to glisten. On the other hand, no one but Andy had ever ridden the stallion. Ragged and broke, here he had the finest horse in the country and no way to feed it!

His spirits brightened. "Say, old boy, how about our looking up that rancher who used to own your mama. What was his name? Allen? Anyone in Moab will know. I'll bet he will be real glad to hear his mare's all safe and sound in that hidden valley." An idea burst full blown. "All those other mares you stole are like gold dust in a poke. Maybe this Allen will lend me some of his hands. We'll drive the herd out, return the mares to their owners, and dicker for the colts and fillies. You're mine, and I reckon I should have some say about what happens to the family you sired."

The closer he got to Moab, the more the idea appealed to him. With the shrewd knowledge of his kind, Andy decided to stop in Moab long enough to see if the storekeeper would give him a change of clothing on credit, then head for Allen's ranch.

His plans met with an abrupt disruption when he got within earshot of Moab. The village he remembered as quiet and a little lazy rang with noise. Something in it put Andy on the alert. He found a good-sized thicket out of town, led Sheik behind it so he stood screened from the road, and tied him. "I'll be back. First, I'm going to see what's causing the commotion."

Mounting Chinquapin, Andy rode into town. Bright bunting and flags tipped him off. "Well, if it ain't Independence Day." A wide grin touched his face. "Some goings-on." He finally got through the crowd and took extra precautions with Chinquapin by tying her to a hitching rail near the store. Although trained to stand with reins dropped, she might bolt from the volume of noise and confusion.

Andy hurried into the store, skirted a swarm of customers who filled the place, and strode to the proprietor. "Any chance of getting some decent clothes on credit?" He saw refusal in the man's eyes and leaned close. "Keep it under your hat, but I caught and broke Sheik. I also know where his band of mares is hiding. Is that good enough for you? I plan to —"

The storekeeper's eyes bulged. He kept his voice low and repeated, "Sheik! Cowboy, is he here in Moab?"

Andy nodded.

"Get what you need, then go get him and enter him in the big race. Here's the entry fee." The man peeled a bill off a roll from his pocket and slipped it into Andy's hand. He whispered, "Don't enter him as Sheik if you want to have some fun. Call him the Mystery Horse."

Andy warmed to the man's excitement. At his benefactor's urging, he selected new pants and shirt, gratefully accepted the offer of a razor and the use of the man's living quarters behind the store, and cleaned himself up. "If I win something, half is yours," he told the beaming man after emerging fresh and clean.

The proprietor shook his head decidedly. "You owe me just for the clothes. I aim to collect big by placing some bets."

Andy frowned. Horse races meant betting, and he hated the idea of making Sheik a reason to gamble. On the other hand, though, he wasn't doing the betting. He soothed his conscience, snaked his way to the open door, and strode onto the porch.

A young woman in a yellow dress walked directly toward him, head turned to look back, hand raised to wave to someone in the crowd. Andy had no time to step aside or alert her to the fact that he stood in front of her. Carried forward by her rapid pace, she bumped into him so hard, she staggered.

"Whoa, Miss." Andy's arms shot out to steady her. She looked up with the softest, bluest eyes he had ever seen. Light brown hair worn in short curls peeped from beneath a becoming hat. Rose pink colored her white cheeks, and Andy Cullen temporarily forgot about Sheik, the race, and everything else in the world except the warm feeling that rushed through him.

In rapid succession, three scowling cowboys appeared, Andy released her and mumbled an explanation, and the girl's laugh chimed like harness bells. Andy tore his gaze from her long enough to shake hands with her watchdogs. He laughed away the spokesman's apology and felt an indescribable sense of loss when a big man appeared, to be led away by the young woman he called Linnet. What a pretty name and how fitting! Only after excusing himself, shoving through the crowd, and climbing back on Chinquapin, did Andy remember that the cowboy had called her Miss Allen. Then that big, belligerent man must be her father, probably the same Allen who owned Sheik's mother. Of all the strange co-incidences. He firmly pushed them out of his mind and rode back to where he'd tethered Sheik, gave him a quick dusting, and left Chinquapin mournfully looking after them from her secure position.

Back into town, then down the street toward the starting point of the race. Men with startled faces fell back from horse and rider. A ripple of amazement swelled into a roar. "That's for you," Andy told Sheik, whose inclination to show off resulted in a series of dancing steps. "Now, I know you've never raced before, but all you have to do is get out in front of the rest of the horses and stay there. There ain't no fancy footwork required, just the fastest run you can man-age."

Sheik snorted and tossed his head. His rider had the feeling the animal knew exactly the part he must play.

"Winning means paying for the clothes plus oats and hay for you," Andy tempted, all the time patting the stallion's neck and keeping a tight rein.

Sheik appeared surprisingly indifferent to the crowd but eyed his compatriots when the ten horses entered in the race lined up, then he tossed his head again.

Crack! The starting pistol fired. Andy's spurless boot heels dug into Sheik's sides. "Go, old boy!"

The stallion's first leap carried him a length ahead of the others and started a volcano-sized roar among the watchers. With the same precision perfected in the long races up and down the hidden valley, Sheik reached the end of the course, wheeled, and headed back far ahead of the swift horses who, by comparison, looked as if they were trotting.

Horse and rider reached the finish line; the roar became a din when they swept across. A hoofbeat later, it changed to horror. A toddling child had somehow escaped her mother's care. She ran on chubby legs into the middle of the street and paused, bewildered by the crowd that had pressed forward to see the finish until only a narrow lane existed.

A flash of yellow brought groans from the watchers. An agonized voice cried, "No!" The next second, the yellow-clad runner flung herself protectively over the child and huddled in the dusty street.

Andy Cullen's range-trained eyes took in the terrible situation. His heart silently pleaded, *Lord, help,* while his cool nerve and iron control screamed he had but one choice. Turning Sheik into the crowd at a dead run meant inevitable death for bystanders. The short distance to the crouched, spread-eagled figure destroyed any hope of reining the stallion in. Sheik's flying hooves would descend like battering rams. Yet the black had not been trained to jump.

The sweat of fear poured down Andy's face. His hands iced but clung to the reins in a death grip. "Now!" He slammed his boot heels into the black flanks and felt the stallion's mighty surge of power. Sheik sprang into the air and over the fallen figures as easily as leaping over a rattlesnake in the trail. He hit the ground far on the other side, still running.

"Thank You, Lord!" Andy cried. Although relief threatened to unseat him, he allowed Sheik to run for a good half mile before pulling him to a walk. "If I never loved you before, I love you now," the disheveled cowboy choked out. He slid from the saddle, put both arms around the lathered horse's neck, and fought the floodwaters gathered just behind his eyelids.

An eternity later, his shaking shoulders stilled. Andy wiped his hot face, mounted Sheik, and slowly rode him back to town. "They can't be hurt," he whispered. "Your hooves didn't even touch her — them." Yet he brushed off the reaching hands and sincere praises of the crowd when he got back to Moab. His gaze turned from side to side, seeking a yellow gown — the right yellow gown, with a laughing face and blue eyes above it.

Andy failed in his mission but at last saw one of the three cowboys who had accosted him earlier. "Miss Allen and the baby. Are they all right?"

Admiration, thankfulness, and gloom filled the tanned face. "The kid's scared but fine." He paused.

"And Miss Allen?"

"Don't know." The cowboy shook his head, and Andy saw misery in his eyes. "They took her to the doc."

"Sheik didn't touch her. Did she get hurt when she threw herself into the road?" A sudden obstruction made it hard to talk. "I never saw such a brave act."

The cowboy squared his shoulders. His jaw set, and he glanced down. His voice sounded hoarse, rough. "A lot braver than you know, Mister. Linnet Allen's the last person in the world who should be pulling stunts like that. Her ticker's no good. She came out to the Rocking A with her daddy from Boston." His face worked. "I hear tell the doctors back East said 'twouldn't make no difference since she was going to die anyway. She's been somewhat better since she came. Now this." He spread his calloused brown hands in a helpless gesture.

Andy felt like he'd been run down by a whole herd of wild horses. That sweet, pretty girl, dying from heart trouble? *No!* He wanted to holler, to grab the cowboy and tell him to stop lying. He could not. The expression on the rider's face showed a truth that could not be denied.

CHAPTER 8

"No!" Linnet fought the darkness, the thunder of hooves, the great black shadow that swept over her. She felt her eardrums would burst from the noise. Just when it became unendurable, the din lessened, only to be replaced with a mighty roar. Too frightened to care, heart pounding, she felt someone lift and carry her. She struggled against the imprisoning arms. "The baby —"

"Scared but safe," a strange, gruff voice answered. The prick of a needle in her arm stilled Linnet's questions, and she drifted into a noiseless, welcome place.

"Well?" George Allen barked the question hovering on Judd's and Mrs. Salt's lips.

The Moab doctor compressed his lips in a straight line. "Can't tell yet. If you men will step outside, I'll have Mrs. Salt undress her so I can do an examination."

Judd looked down at the slight, pale figure

of his daughter. "How could she do it?" he cried. His voice broke.

The crusty doctor cleared his throat. "From what I've seen of the young lady, she couldn't stand by and see a child in danger. I understand she stood closest to the street?"

"We put her there so she could see the race better," George told him. His face worked, but the doctor shooed him out, along with Judd. The brothers didn't talk. Even now Linnet could be dying.

At last, George managed to say, "If she doesn't make it, God forbid, she gave her life to save another."

"Don't!" Judd buried his face in his hands, and his shoulders heaved. George laid a strong arm over them and simply hung on.

What seemed a lifetime later, the doctor jerked open the door separating his little waiting room from the examining area. Mrs. Salt's beaming face told the story even before the worthy doctor spoke.

"I can't see she's any the worse for her little escapade," the physician informed them. His face wrinkled. "I also can't find much that's irregular about her heart. Rapid pulse just now, of course, but that's to be expected under the circumstances." He beetled his brows over keen eyes. "How long has it been since she's been checked?"

"Several weeks, actually." Judd tried to remember. "Once she made up her mind to come out here and gained in strength, she scoffed at the idea of going back to the doctors." His face grayed. "They'd already pronounced her death sentence, so Linnet said she couldn't see that it mattered what she did."

"Hmm." The doctor stroked his waistcoat, then tapped a pudgy finger against his lips. "I don't want to be premature, but . . . what's she been doing since then?"

Mrs. Salt outlined the program of rest, exercise, and good food. "I also keep her busy sewing," she added. Genuine love flashed in her blue eyes. "When a body's working for someone else's good, it leaves less time to think on her own miseries."

The doctor sent her a look of approval. "Keep up the good work," he advised. "Then bring her back to me in a couple of months. Right now I want her to sleep until she wakes up on her own. By the way, who's the rider with brains enough to control his horse? If he'd tried to veer or stop, I'll wager the black would have either trampled her and the child or charged into the crowd and sent me some badly mangled citizens."

George Allen shook his head. "All I know is that his stallion's the mirror image of my Arabian mare stolen awhile back by the leader of a wild horse band. From what I've heard, either the black is Sheik or I'll eat my hat!" He gripped the doctor's hand with his strong paw. "Mrs. Salt, I know you'll want to stay with Linnet. Judd, we have to go find that cowboy and shake his hand." He strode toward the door.

"Thank you." Judd wiped wet eyes and followed, leaving the frankly rejoicing Mrs. Salt and the doctor to tend to their business.

The Allen brothers didn't have to go far to find the hero of the day. A few paces outside the doctor's office, a lithe cowboy leading a black stallion still bearing traces of lather from his magnificent performance hurried toward them. "Mr. Allen, the crowd said your daughter —"

"My niece. This is her father," George interrupted. "She's going to be all right. In fact, she's going to be better than all right unless Doc has taken leave of his senses."

"Thank God!" Andy felt a mountain-sized load slide from his heart. "I knew Sheik didn't touch her, but one of your cowhands said she had a weak heart."

Judd's hand shot out to the young rider

134

whose ripe corn hair hung over his worried brown eyes. "Thanks be to God, the doctor thinks there's a good chance she may recover. It's almost too much to hope for. The only reason we came to Utah was because it didn't matter either way where we lived. Every physician pronounced my daughter's case hopeless."

"Except the Great Physician." Andy looked straight into the distraught man's eyes. A flicker of recognition that a bond lay between them sent joy into the cowboy's heart. He turned to George and said frankly, "Now that I've seen your niece, you may find it hard to believe, but I was on my way to see you when I rode into town and found all the goings-on." He laughed, a clear, ringing sound that tilted the other men's lips up. "I'd been so busy catching and taming Sheik that I forgot the date."

"Where did you find him?" George's eyes gleamed, and he reached out to pat the stallion's neck. Quicker than lightning, Sheik jerked his head back and reared.

"It's all right, old boy." Andy's iron grip brought his horse under control and brought looks of admiration from the Allens, plus Reddy Hode, Tommy Blake, and Charlie Moore, who had followed in Andy and Sheik's wake. "Sorry," Andy apologized.

"So far he's only used to me."

"I have a feeling he's a one-man horse and always will be," Reddy ventured. "Good thing. I ain't no horse thief, but that animal's enough to tempt even an honest cowpoke like me." His sally brought laughter.

"Mr. Allen, I'd like to talk with you in private," Andy quietly said. "Begging your pardon, boys."

"Of course. But anything you say should be to my brother as well as me. He's the new half owner of the Rocking A."

"That's swell." Andy could have said a lot more about Judd's pretty daughter and how relief had run hot and swift through his veins when he heard the good news concerning her health. As soon as the three hands ambled off, joshing Andy with remarks about being willing to take Sheik off his hands anytime, the cowboy squared his shoulders and lowered his voice. He told his story well, from the moment he first heard of Sheik and dreamed about capturing him, to the thrilling and terrifying moment when he discovered the stallion putting up his final, losing battle against the slide.

"I never felt sorrier for any critter than that horse, cutting himself on sharp rocks, trying to get free," he said. Without glorifying himself, he hurried over the actual rescue and breaking. His heart pounded with the same excitement he'd experienced when Sheik at last gave in.

"And that ain't all," he finished. "I rolled rocks so the mares — including one that must be your Arabian, Mr. Allen — and colts and fillies would stay in the valley until someone comes for them."

"Where is this valley?" George demanded, then laughed at his own eagerness. "Whoa, first you'll want to be dickering, I suppose."

"I figure the ranchers who get their mares back will be glad enough to have them so's we can make a deal," Andy said. "Sheik's mine, by right of finding and breaking. The colts and fillies sired by Sheik are a bonus. They ought to be worth quite a bit for that reason."

"I can see you've thought it all out." George considered for a moment. "What do you want for them?"

"I need your hands to help me drive," Andy told him. His brown eyes sparkled in anticipation. "I've got one of the best cow ponies in the West, plus having Sheik along will encourage the herd to follow. I know I can trust you. I don't know the other ranchers around here. Once they give their word, will they keep it? I'll return the mares to their rightful owners. Any unbranded animals, and that's all the colts and fillies, will be for sale at the going price."

"That's more than fair," George admitted. He frowned. "Only rancher who may kick up a storm and try to claim some of the offspring is Silas Dunn of the Bar D. He'll be outvoted, though. You found the horses. They're yours. Say, what's your name, anyway, and where are you from?"

"Andy Cullen, lately of Arizona. Rode last for the Double J near Flagstaff."

George grunted. "I've heard of them and all good. How'd you like to throw in with me? Judd and I could use another good rider. Top wages and best food in Utah, as well as one of the prettiest ranches."

"I'd like that," Andy told him. He hesitated, then said, "One thing. It won't be forever. I aim to stash away what I get on this deal and have a spread of my own sometime. Mr. Allen, what's the best way to go about bringing the horses out of the canyon? I've got a feeling it ain't smart to leave them there too long." He repeated the conversation he'd overheard in the Moab cafe weeks earlier.

George acted dumbfounded. "Drive them onto the Point and fence it? Who'd think up such an idea as that?"

Andy faithfully described the three men whose faces he had seen. "I couldn't see the one with his back to me, but he had broad shoulders and spoke clearly and slowly."

George shook his head. "Could be any of a half-dozen ranch owners. Anything to distinguish some of the others? They sound like all cowmen."

"No, but the three scoundrels who relieved me of food and saddlebags and blanket made a deep impression." Andy quickly related the story of his holdup. "One of them had strange eyes, almost colorless. I'd recognize them again, even though the ornery skunk's hat shaded them. The leader had a pleasant laugh. The third got knocked down by my mare, Chinquapin, and it tickled the leader. I guess I should be thankful they didn't put a hole in me and leave me there. Oh, they stole my bedroll, too, and Chinq's blanket. I hated to lose that. It was a Christmas present from my pards at the Double J. The boss's wife put a little *A* in one corner." He grinned. "I got a hunch someday I'm going to see that saddle blanket. When I do, I can track down who robbed me."

George leaned closer, a mysterious glint in his eyes. "Cullen, could the man with the pleasant laugh and the wide-shouldered gent in the cafe have been the same person?"

Andy considered, then regretfully shook his head. "No. Why?"

George compressed his lips. "Just curious. Now, about the horse drive, I suggest we call together all the ranchers around here who have lost mares the last several years. We'll put your deal up to them, tell them we need hands from every spread represented to help drive, and set up a fair way of selling the unbranded stock. Draw lots with number one getting first choice, and so on. Or, don't you want to keep some? Plenty of room on the Rocking A.

"You sure don't want to geld Sheik," George exploded.

"Never!" Andy thought of the proud stallions who had either died or had become spiritless after gelding. "I'll turn him back onto the range before that."

"Don't blame you a bit." George dropped a heavy hand to the younger man's shoulder. "I have a section that's not being used. We'll put Sheik and any unbranded mares in his band there, away from the rest of the stock." He downed the obstacle, and a shrewd expression came to his face. "Reckon it won't hurt none to put on paper exactly how this horse drive and trading are going to be. I'll sign it first, and we won't have any trouble with the others . . . except maybe Dunn, as I said." He shrugged. "He can be sweeter than apple pie sometimes and sourer than green apples others."

Sheik had grown restive during the long confab. Now he tossed his head and shinnied, clearly jealous of these strangers who took so much of his new master's attention. Andy absently patted him. "I'd better go collect my prize money and pay off the storekeeper for my duds. Have to get Chinq, too, before she thinks I've deserted her." He started to move away but stopped when the door of the doctor's office opened. A short, brown-haired woman with blue eyes and a nice smile stood in the doorway.

"How is she?" Judd Allen, who had listened but made no effort to enter the conversation, sprang toward the woman.

"Now, Mr. Judd, there's no need to worry. She's fine. Awake and asking for you. She also wants to see the cowboy who owns the black horse. That's you, I reckon."

Andy felt her single glance had weighed him and learned everything about him there was to know. He rapidly revised his first estimate of her as just a sweet lady. "Yes, Ma'am." He bared his head and held his Stetson in his free hand.

"Well, don't just stand there. Come in."

141

Andy looked helplessly around. Would Sheik suffer himself to be held by one of the men? Undoubtedly not after his little dance earlier. Andy's quick look spotted a sturdy cottonwood nearby. He led Sheik to it and tied him securely before following the woman inside the waiting room. "I'm Mrs. Salt. Don't stay more than a few minutes," she warned. To his surprise, she laid a hand on Judd Allen's sleeve and said, "Let him go first," then opened the door to the examining room, ushered Andy in, and closed the door behind him.

A keen-eyed doctor with bushy eyebrows stood next to the bed. "You are —"

"Andy Cullen. Mrs. Salt said Miss Allen wanted to see me." He advanced to where the girl lay on a white-sheeted high bed. Her blue eyes looked enormous in her pale face, and short brown curls made a halo around it.

"I . . . I'm glad you are all right," he stammered, twisting his big hat in his hands.

"You!" She tried to sit up, but the doctor pushed her back against the flat pillow.

"Just take it easy, Miss Allen," he warned. "You're going to be fine. Your daddy's waiting to come in."

"I didn't know . . . the child, that horse . . ." She covered her lips with trembling fingers. "How did you keep from k-killing us?"

"Sheik leaped clean over you both," Andy told her.

"What a grand horse! May I see him sometime?" Pink banners streamed into her face.

"Of course." He wanted to tell her how he'd caught Sheik, that he'd be at the Rocking A before she reached home, and a hundred other things.

The doctor forestalled him. "Later. Send her father in on your way out, please."

Andy's contagious grin and conspiratorial look brought an answering smile from the patient. "Right, Doc. So long for now, Miss Allen." He ducked his head and marched out but not before he heard the doctor say, "Cocky young rooster, but I kind of like him."

To Andy's everlasting regret, the door closed before he caught the young woman's reply.

"Cullen, do you plan to stick around for the rest of the doings?" George Allen's voice boomed and brought Andy out of his meditations concerning young ladies and yellow dresses.

"Ump-umm. If it's all the same to you, I'll go get my winnings, rub down Sheik, collect Chinq, and head for the Rocking A."

"Good. Soon as Linnet's able, we'll be on our way, too. If you get there before we do, make yourself to home. Most of the boys are in town and will probably stay over, including the cook, but there's plenty of grub, and you look to me like a man who can take care of himself."

"I fry a mean hunk of meat," Andy bragged. "Give me that and a biscuit, and I'm fine." The desire to be totally honest with his new employer made him add, "Besides, now that I won the race, I'll stoke up with a good meal at the cafe. I've been pretty empty the last couple of days."

George's quick grin showed he appreciated the candor. "Nothing wrong with being broke and hungry; I've been that way myself," he gruffly said. "Any chance you want me to carry most of your winnings to the ranch?"

Andy flushed. Anger overcame caution. He drew himself to full height. "I don't drink or gamble or worse."

George's face turned scarlet. "I didn't think you did. The reason I offered is, there's a lot of strangers in Moab and some not so strange. They all saw you win the race."

The significance of it dawned on the new

Rocking A hand. "Sorry, Sir. I'll go get the money." He turned away. Even his ears felt hot at the way he'd misjudged the hearty rancher.

"I like a man who sticks up for himself, Cullen. No need to apologize. You might kind of mention around you aren't carrying the prize money."

The veiled warning rang in Andy's brain on the long walk down the main street. Dozens of men had crowded into the saloon where he had to go for his money. A loud cheer rose when he entered. "Hey, Cowboy, that's some horse!"

Andy recognized the storekeeper's voice and quickly located the beaming man. "Thanks," Andy said.

"Set 'em up," the man said. "Drinks on me. I ain't never made such a killing off you boys as today. C'mon, Cowboy, and drink to the grandest stallion what's ever rode down Main Street!"

Andy thought fast, then his wide, white grin appeared. "Sure, if you've got any lemonade."

"Lemonade! What d'you want lemonade for? That's no man's drink," the bartender growled.

Andy stepped closer. A lock of hair fell to his forehead. He grinned again. "That so?

Mighty peculiar, ain't it? I'd have bet anything no one but a real man could ride Sheik . . . and win." He clenched his hands, hoping humor would save the situation. It did. First the storekeeper, then the bartender grinned sheepishly and allowed as how he was right. Andy downed an oversized glass of frosty lemonade and drawled, "Where's my prize money?"

"Right here." The storekeeper handed over a wad of bills, some of them dirty, others wrinkled but big enough to choke Sheik and Chinq together. "What you going to do with it? Order more lemonade?"

The good-natured crowd roared, but Andy laughed, peeled off what he owed for his clothes, took a couple dollars from the roll, stuck them in his pocket, then announced, "My new boss, Mr. Allen, said he'd keep it for me." He turned an innocent face toward the men gathered around him. "I'm just keeping enough out to get me the biggest steak in Moab. Safer, that way. Why, if I kept it with me, I might buy out the store." In the midst of laughter, he escaped, stopped on the boardwalk in front of the saloon, and mopped his hot face. *Whew!* That had been close. His Trail Pard must have kept the men friendly even when Andy refused to drink. He'd seen what booze did to men and wanted no part of it, ever.

A dozen horses hitched to the rail shied nervously when shots came from down the street. *Cowboys letting off steam,* Andy thought. The horses reared again. One in particular acted determined to break free and flee.

Andy stepped nearer. "Whoa, Boy," he told the frightened sorrel. The mare quieted under his touch. Andy's eyes gleamed at her saddle and trappings. Pretty and polished to a high gloss. He leaned closer. Froze. A bit of the saddle blanket hung lower on one side than the other. In its corner was a tiny, telltale *A.*

CHAPTER 9

"Hold it!" A voice rang from behind Andy. He felt something hard poke into his back, and he slowly turned. A broad-shouldered man with drooping mustache ordered, "Now suppose you tell us what you think you're doing with that horse."

Steel met steel. "Suppose *you* tell *me* why this sorrel mare's wearing my saddle blanket." Andy's brown eyes darkened, and he crouched a bit.

"Are you calling me a thief?" His opponent sheathed his revolver and doubled his fists. A little ripple of shock ran through the crowd of onlookers who had laughed with Andy and now turned hostile.

"I'm saying three skunks held me up and took my grub and bedroll, saddlebags, and blanket."

"Hey, what's going on?" A burly man elbowed through the crowd. "Dunn, what're you bellyaching about now?"

"I caught this rider examining my horse real careful-like and called him on it. Now, he's accusing me of stealing a saddle blanket." His laugh rang out contemptuously.

Andy caught the glint of a silver star before the newcomer retorted, "Silas, you'd be more likely to steal his horse if you could get away with it. This is the young feller who just won the race on the black stallion that everyone's saying is Sheik."

Dunn's mouth dropped open. He jerked as if hit by a speeding bullet. *"You?"* Greed glittered in his eyes. "What will you take for him, providing he's really Sheik."

"He is, but he ain't for sale." Andy whipped back toward the sheriff. "The sorrel's wearing my saddle blanket. What are you going to do about it?"

The sheriff shoved his sombrero back on his sandy hair. "Well, now, stealing's a serious charge. Can you prove the blanket's yours? What I can see of it, it looks a heap like any other saddle blanket."

"You'll find a tiny embroidered *A* worked into one corner," Andy said quietly. "My pards on the Double J in Arizona gave me the blanket for Christmas, and the boss's wife put my initial on it."

"There ain't no *A* or any other letter on that blanket," Dunn bawled. His face contorted with anger. "Even if there is, and like I said, there ain't, this tinhorn coulda seen it when he was snooping around."

The sheriff ignored the rancher's rantings, strode to the sorrel, lifted the edge of the blanket, and examined it. "It's here all right." He gave Dunn a measuring glance. "And unless a feller knew what to look for, he'd have to have mighty sharp eyes to see it." Dunn bellowed, and the sheriff cut him short with a scathing look. "You just stated clear and positive there was no such thing, so you must never have seen it. Unsaddle the mare and give him his blanket."

Dunn just stood there, speechless with rage. Dark, unhealthy red suffused his face, and storm clouds gathered in his eyes. Andy took an extra long look, expecting them to be colorless. They were not. Dark and dangerous looking, those eyes did not belong to any of the three men who had jumped and robbed him months earlier.

"Move, Dunn, or I'll run you in. Maybe I will, anyway. How'd you get this partic'lar saddle blanket?"

Dunn spat into the dust of the street. "Won it playing poker."

The sheriff's voice turned gravelly. "From a man just passing through, I s'pose."

Sardonic humor ended in a sneer. "How'd

you get so smart, Sheriff? That's just who he was. I cleaned him out —"

"I'll just bet you did," the sheriff interrupted.

"Like I said, I cleaned him. He still wanted to play and offered me this blanket." Dunn sent a venomous look at Andy. "I obliged him. Didn't consider it my business where he got it."

Andy accurately gauged the lack of love between the two and tucked the knowledge away. It might come in handy sometime.

"Get that saddle off. Now!" The sheriff's words cracked like a bullwhip. "Cowboy, if I were you, I'd wash it before putting it on a great horse like that Sheik of yours. No telling what kind of vermin it's been around."

The crowd howled, swung into sympathy for the newcomer to Moab who had shown up Dunn in front of his cronies. Evidently, the big rancher was no favorite among them, either.

Andy glanced from their mirth-filled faces back to Dunn, who sullenly marched over to the sorrel. His eyes widened. Those same shoulders had been turned square to him in the Moab cafe the fateful day he overheard the plan to drive Sheik and his band onto Dead Horse Point and fence them in.

Still angry over the saddle blanket business, he opened his mouth to blurt out the scheme but thought better of it. His friend Smokey back in Arizona had once grinned and said, "Pard, the way I see it is like this. The good Lord musta purely wanted us to do twice as much listening as talking, or He wouldn't have given us two ears an' only one mouth."

Now, Andy buttoned his lip, decided he'd keep both ears open, and see what happened.

Saddle blanket over his left arm, aware of the baleful look Dunn gave him, Andy shook hands with the sheriff. "Thanks."

"Who are you, anyway?" the official wanted to know. "All Moab knows about you is that you ride in here on the grandest horse in southeastern Utah, win the race, keep Sheik from killing a mighty brave young woman, and brace Dunn. Oh, yeah, you mentioned riding for the Double J. Most of us in these parts have heard of that spread." He eyed Andy with twinkling, half-closed eyes.

"Name's Andy Cullen, and you know 'most all that's important, except Mr. Dunn's going to be mighty surprised when my new boss, George Allen, fires off our big plan." He chuckled at the sheriff's expression and worked his way through the laughing crowd.

A voice at his elbow drawled, "I sure do admire a feller who stands up for what's his."

A second and third chimed in, "Me, too."

Andy turned his head. The three cowboys who'd leaped to Linnet's defense kept pace with him, grinning like three demons.

"Say, is it true you're hiring on with us?" the leader asked.

Andy stopped short. "Think I should?"

"You bet! Now maybe we can stop some of the —"

Andy's keen gaze saw the quick dig of an elbow in the speaker's ribs and refrained from asking questions. He'd have to prove his trustworthiness by more than winning races and facing Silas Dunn before he could expect the hands' confidences or loyalty. Yet, by the time the quartet reached the cottonwood where Sheik indignantly proclaimed his displeasure at being forsaken, even temporarily, Andy had sorted out names and faces and suspected Reddy Hode, Tommy Blake, and Charlie Moore to be true-blue to their employer and tickled to death over the events of the day. After he turned over the bulk of his winnings to George Allen, Andy realized his belt buckle felt like it was rubbing his spine from hunger. Still, he took time to conscientiously rub down the black, go get Chinq, and threaten the old man at the livery stable with death and destruction if he let anything happen to either horse.

Less than an hour later, Andy rode out of Moab astride the proud stallion with faithful Chinq trotting close behind. Prime roast beef, mashed potatoes and gravy, hot biscuits, vegetables, and two pieces of apple pie lay tucked in his belly and fortified him for the trip to the Rocking A. Lulled by Sheik's easy motion and the waning heat of the day, he reviewed everything that had happened from the time he first caught sight of flags and buntings. "Seems like a week ago." He yawned. "Not just this morning."

His mind turned to his meeting with Linnet Allen outside the store, and a smile stretched his lips. It died when he relived the chilling moment he saw her fling herself over the toddler directly in his and Sheik's path. Again a wave of gratitude surged through him. "Thanks, Lord." Andy hunkered down in the saddle, alert to anything unusual but comfortable and relaxed.

A thunder of hooves roused him from his reverie. He glanced back. Three men on racing horses pounded down the rutted road behind him, bent low over their mounts' necks. Friend or foe? Andy didn't wait to find out. He leaned forward and touched his heels to Sheik's sides. No horse in Moab could match the black's speed, even after his earlier run. "Go, Boy. Come on, Chinq."

Sheik cannoned into a mighty leap and settled into a dead run. Wind whistled by Andy's ears, yet his excellent hearing caught the steady drum of Chinquapin's racing feet, then a stentorian, "Cullen! Wait up."

Andy laughed aloud and gradually reined the stallion to a stop. He turned and waited for the three riders who had tried so unsuccessfully to catch him. When they pulled up, he laughed again. "What took you boys so long?"

Reddy Hode expertly controlled his fractious horse; Tommy Blake and Charlie Moore did the same. "Why's you running away from us?" Reddy disgustedly burst out. "How are we s'posed to escort you home when you're riding a critter like that?" He pointed accusingly at Sheik.

"How was I s'posed to know you weren't horse thieves?" Andy mimicked. "This *critter* would be mighty fine pickings for a rustler."

"Sure, 'cept we ain't no rustlers. Moab done quieted down 'cause of the near accident. Miss Allen's better, and her daddy and uncle are bringing her home. We figured we'd mosey on back, too." Reddy's crooked grin reminded Andy of himself after he first met Smokey Travis and the Rocking A riders — curious, friendly, a mite cautious.

"I'm sure glad she's all right," Andy said from his heart.

"So're we. Soon as she gets real strong, we're gonna convince her this part of Utah's the best place on earth for staying healthy," Tommy put in.

"Yeah. She needs to settle down, find a handsome cowpoke to marry, and make some feller the sweetest little wife in the West," Reddy added.

"It won't be you," Charlie smirked. "There ain't nothing purty or han'some about you at all."

"I'm better looking than some I could mention," Reddy said significantly. "And at least I ain't old enough to be her daddy."

"Like the owner of the Bar D?"

Charlie's mocking question snapped Andy's head up. That bullish rancher, courting a delicate flower like Linnet Allen? "Impossible!" he burst out.

Reddy cocked a knowing head. "Naw. I saw him looking at her just before she run out into the street." His lips turned down in scorn. "Sure didn't see him make no effort to save either her or the kid, and he was standing there, bold and barefaced, in the front of the crowd."

"How come you noticed him?" Tommy asked curiously.

"I make it my business to keep an eye peeled toward anyone who might bother our new boss lady." Reddy gave Andy a look of pure mischief and grinned companionably. " 'Course, sometimes things ain't the way they look, at first, but —" He straightened in the saddle. "With Dunn, it's worth observing."

"Let's hit the trail," Tommy complained. "Now that our new hand's decided we ain't no horse stealers maybe we can ride peaceful-like and not have to eat his horses' dust."

"Say, if you don't mind my asking, how'd you catch Sheik?" Reddy, who had crowded in next to Sheik and forced his comrades to drop just behind when the road wouldn't permit four abreast, sounded more eager than curious.

"Talk loud," Tommy pleaded. "So's we can hear. We don't dare get too close to Sheik's heels."

Andy had already decided how trustworthy the three hands were and frankly told them the whole story. Encouraged by their respectful silence broken only by a wild "Yippee-ay" at the end of his recital, he outlined his plan for rounding up Sheik's band and how he planned to return the stolen mares but sell colts, fillies, and any other unbranded horses.

"Did you happen to notice any Bar D brands on them?" Reddy's question sounded just a mite too casual.

"I kept too busy with Sheik to pay attention to brands," Andy frankly said. "Why?"

"Dunn's grabby. Don't let him buffalo you into turning over what ain't his." The next moment, Reddy changed the subject, leaving Andy to ponder the warning.

The riders traveled the last few miles engaged in desultory conversation that ranged from the size of the Rocking A to how well Allen treated his hands. By the time they reached the home corral, Andy felt he had a good idea of what to expect.

"Where can I put Sheik so he won't pick a fight?" he inquired, after tending to his horses. "Allen said he had a section he wasn't using."

"We'll show you." All three cowboys insisted on riding with the new hand to a choice chunk of land that boasted shade and water. "The boss just sold off a bunch of horses and hasn't run others in yet," the loquacious Reddy offered. "Leave that pretty little mare, and Sheik should be all right. There's plenty of space for him to roam and strong fences, although if he took a notion to jump them, he probably could. 'Tain't reasonable he will want to leave feed and water and his girlfriend unless something spooks him. Come on. We can ride double back to the corral."

A quiver of unknown origin flicked Andy. He rubbed Sheik's head, then Chinquapin's. Why did he feel so reluctant to ride off behind Reddy? Realization left him ruefully grinning. Outside of a few short absences in town, tonight was the first time he'd been apart from Sheik since he rode into the canyon and discovered the trapped horse. Andy shook his head at his fancies and chided himself. Yet the same feeling nagged him while he got settled in an empty bunk in the spacious bunkhouse and drifted off to sleep.

Long before daybreak, he slipped into his clothes and, stocking-footed and carrying his boots, stepped outside into a murky dawn. Taking care not to disturb his companions, he eased his way to the corral, snatched a lariat coiled around a post, and snagged one of the horses milling around.

159

Something within shouted *Hurry,* and he urged the horse to its utmost.

When they reached the pasture, Andy pulled the borrowed animal to a stop and peered ahead. Daylight crept over the red rocks that made a natural wall on two sides.

Andy whistled. Waited. No response. He whistled again, then rode forward. "Sheik. Chinq," he called.

Sheik. Chinq, the walls faithfully echoed.

Alarmed beyond belief, he pressed forward, following the uneven fence until —

"No!" The denial thundered back and forth between the cliffs, accusing and confirming the sight Andy longed to shut out but couldn't. A section of fence lay flat, either torn down by humans or knocked over by flying hooves of jumping horses.

Heart in his mouth, Andy jumped from the saddle, secured his horse, and leaped to the outside of the downed fence. He stared at the ground. Some of his dread vanished when he found no boot tracks. Just fresh signs of two strong horses on their way to freedom. He tore has gaze from the ground, heart heavy, remembering how he had hoped Chinquapin would never have to choose between Sheik and her master.

Now she had chosen. Her smaller tracks showed clear, along with the deeper, larger imprints of the stallion.

Andy longed to mount and go after them, then shook his head. Not on this horse. He could never begin to catch them. Better to go back, rouse Reddy and Tommy and Charlie, then get a faster horse. He'd have to let the Allens know, as well. He pictured George's jaw dropping when he heard the bad news.

Andy sighed and followed on foot several paces in the direction the tracks led. Hope refilled his heart. With the unexplainable instinct the Creator had placed in Sheik, the stallion's tracks led straight in the direction of the now-sealed canyon and the band of horses waiting to be freed.

"We can take a shortcut and go directly there," Andy shouted. Moments later, he had remounted and goaded the Rocking A horse back toward the ranch buildings.

Linnet roused from a deep slumber to a commotion in the corral. She struggled from bed and ran to the window, marveling at how alert and strong she felt. Ever since the doctor gruffly told her he believed that, in time, her heart would be healed, she had thanked God in advance for that day and taken in deep breaths of the clear air. Uncle George had insisted on borrowing a horse to ride home, leaving Judd to drive with Mrs. Salt next to him and Linnet stretched out on the backseat of the contraption. "No sense overdoing it," he'd told her. "What happened today was enough to set anyone back, and we don't want to spoil the good progress you've made so far."

She had actually been grateful and slept a good deal of the way. When they got home, Mrs. Salt ordered her to bed, brought her supper on a tray, and grimly watched her eat every bite. "Thank the good Lord you're here and not trampled under that wicked horse's hooves," she announced.

"He isn't wicked." Linnet put down her fork. "He must be intelligent and wonderful to leap over me like that." She pushed the empty tray away. "Let's not talk about it."

"All right." Mrs. Salt acted subdued. "Did Mr. Allen or Mr. Judd tell you they hired that young cowboy?"

Linnet wondered why the news should make her heart jump. "No."

"Well, they did. And that isn't all." She dropped to a chair near the bed and told the listening young woman how their new hand had gotten away with drinking lemonade in the saloon and making Silas Dunn look like a fool in front of the whole town. "Andy Cullen sure made an impression on

Moab today. Got his blanket back, too, and without a killing."

Linnet felt the blood drain from her face. "Surely a man wouldn't kill for a saddle blanket!" Her eyes widened with horror.

"Dunn might. When he comes calling, and he will, keep out of sight as much as you can."

Bewildered, Linnet could only stammer, "But why?"

Mrs. Salt's lips closed in a thin line before she opened them enough to mutter, "There have been stories about him trying to marry every woman in the country, decent or not."

"Is he handsome?"

"Hardly!" Mrs. Salt snorted, and her eyes flashed. "I'd as soon have a loco coyote hanging around as him. He's nearer my age than yours, but that won't make any difference."

Linnet giggled. "Is he bowlegged?"

"Not so you'd notice. Why'd you ask such a question?" Mrs. Salt threw her hands into the air.

Filled with the joy of returning to health and the promise of a future, Linnet told how she and her father had laughed over their coming west and how he predicted a bowlegged cowboy would be her fate.

"My, my, I wouldn't have thought it of

163

Mr. Judd." A smile lurked in the corners of her mouth and softened her eyes. She smoothed the pillows, straightened Linnet's bedclothes, and bade her good night and a peaceful sleep. But just before she stepped into the hall and closed the door behind her, Mrs. Salt fired a parting shot. "By the way, our new hand with the black stallion isn't a bit bowlegged. He walks as straight and proud as your daddy and uncle." The door clicked, and the convulsed girl heard the housekeeper-cook's firm footsteps echo down the hall and fade into silence.

Linnet laughed until she cried, then fell into a sound sleep to dream of powerful black horses, laughing cowboys, and a masked man who came to call and said his name was Silas Dunn.

Now she stood by her window, wishing she knew why cowboys ran to the corral, saddled horses, and called to each other. The Rocking A always rose early, but something in the very air hinted at an unusual situation. Linnet hastily donned a housecoat, thrust her feet into slippers, and stepped into the hall. "Mrs. Salt?"

The good woman appeared as if by magic. Excitement oozed from her. "I knew those pesky men would wake you."

"What's happening?"

Mrs. Salt smoothed her huge apron down over her work dress. "Both of Andy Cullen's horses have bolted. The men are going after them. Cullen should have known he couldn't trust Sheik. This isn't the first time he's run off with a mare, and I'll wager it won't be the last."

Forgetting her attire, Linnet lightly ran down the stairs. Life on the ranch certainly differed from the sheltered eastern existence she had known. She giggled, thinking of the expression proper Bostonians would wear if suddenly awakened by the sound of horses beneath their windows.

CHAPTER 10

Unwilling to miss the drama taking place in the corral, Linnet hurried to a window and flung it open to the early July morning. She clutched her housecoat close and from the frail protection of a spotless curtain peered out. The clear air amplified voices, and she could hear the conversation very well.

"Wait, boys." George Allen's bellow stilled the hubbub. "There's no sense in rushing off shorthanded." A cry of protest went up from the vastly depleted number of Rocking A riders. George raised his voice to a roar. "Hold it. We know where the horses are headed. It won't take more than half a day to notify the other ranchers of what's going on. They'll be here late this afternoon with as many hands as they can spare. We'll leave tomorrow morning."

"Aw, Boss, it's a pure shame to let Sheik and that pretty little chestnut mare get a day's start," one of the cowboys called.

Linnet felt sure it was Reddy who had spoken.

A mumble of agreement ran through the grouped men.

"What's a day?" George asked reasonably, his voice diminished but still plenty loud. "When Sheik gets to the valley and finds he can't get in, he isn't going to up and leave. He'll hang around trying to find a way in. Cullen says there's a goodly bunch of horses holed up in that valley. We're going to need more men than we have here to drive them. The rest of our own outfit will be rolling in this evening, too. We'll head out at daybreak."

"You're the boss, but I ain't too happy about it," the cowboy Linnet had identified as Reddy retorted.

"Everything will be fine, Hode. You boys get some breakfast and start riding to the ranches; one of you swing back by Moab. Better yet, hit town first. You can catch a lot of the ranch owners before they start for home." He turned on his heel and came back toward the house.

Fascinated, Linnet watched his easy stride, then gripped the curtain when a slim rider followed George to the porch.

"Sir, I'd like to go after my horses now and not wait for the others."

Allen wheeled to face his newest hand. "Any special reason?"

From her vantage point, Linnet saw the way Andy Cullen hesitated, then looked square into her uncle's eyes. "I have a funny feeling." His brown eyes pleaded, but he snapped his mouth shut.

"What kind of feeling?"

"I can't explain it, but it has something to do with Sheik and Chinq needing me."

"Go ahead, then. We'll meet you at the valley. Tell me again how to get there."

Andy quickly gave directions. The watching young woman wished with all her heart she could ride out with him to find the black stallion. When the cowboy moved purposefully toward the corral, followed by her uncle's orders to pick whatever horse he wanted, Linnet ran to the front door and confronted her uncle George when he stepped inside. "Could I go?"

"No!" Mrs. Salt whisked into the room, a scandalized expression on her face. "A horse drive's no place for a woman, even one who's a lot stronger than you are."

"Uncle George?" Mutiny rose in Linnet's heart.

"Sorry, Lass." Genuine regret filled his kindly eyes. "Isn't it enough that the doctor's given you hope to get well?"

Shame swept into her heart. Her head drooped like a poorly broken filly's. "I'm sorry. It's just that —"

"That you have Allen blood in you and a pioneering spirit," her father put in from behind her. "I'll stay with you, if you like."

She sensed his longing, even greater than her own. "You'll do no such thing! I want you to help drive the horses and remember all the things that happen so you can tell me. Uncle George will be too busy to notice."

"So you expect me to be a slacker and just watch and let the others do all the work?" Judd drew himself up in mock indignation, and his blue eyes, so like hers, sparkled with fun.

"You know I didn't mean that." The sound of hooves drew her back to the window. This time she dared to draw aside the curtain, heedless of being seen. At that exact moment, Andy Cullen glanced toward the house. Linnet couldn't read his expression, but the wide smile couldn't be denied. He swung aboard the horse he'd just saddled, tipped his hat in her direction, and rode away, leaving her breathless, with a little prayer in her heart for his safety.

The same unexplainable feeling that had

urged him to go after his horses and not wait for the outfit sent Andy pell-mell over the range and back the way he had come a few days earlier. The memory of a young woman's sweet face, framed by a window curtain, rode with him, but the frisky horse that had lolled around the corral while the outfit whooped it up in town required attention. Andy had chosen her not only for her spirit but as bait. Another stallion meant trouble, but a mare offered a lure he hoped Sheik would find irresistible.

In a far shorter time than he'd made on his way to Moab, Andy reached the entrance to the hidden, blocked canyon. Sheik and Chinquapin's clear trail showed that in spite of a shortcut Andy took, they remained ahead of him. He reined in and slipped from the saddle. Hope died. A jumble of foot and hoofprints showed clearly in the thick dust of the trail — and the sheltering rocks he had rolled to block its entrance lay scattered into heaps!

Fearing the worst, Andy looped his mount's reins over a nearby rock and ran through the narrow passage. He halted at the valley entrance and stood transfixed. The rock barricade he had so painstakingly built, no longer existed. He raced into the valley and called. His only response came from a winging eagle. The band of horses had vanished as completely as if a giant hand had scooped them up and transported them to another place.

"Sheik. Chinq," he cried in desperation.

Sheik. Chinq, the rock walls faithfully echoed, then silence again reigned.

"Someone must have heard the horses and figured out their whereabouts," Andy surmised. He shoved his Stetson back and stared at the empty valley. "But where's Sheik? And Chinq?" He tried to crawl into the stallion's mind and figure what he'd do in his place. "Track them. He won't stand for his family being spirited away any more than he stood for being corralled with them out here," Andy decided.

He retraced his steps through the passageway and untied his horse. As much as he longed to head after the herd, she needed rest. He led the protesting animal into the valley and let her drink long and graze. She deserved it. Hat over his eyes, Andy lay prone under the cottonwoods where he'd once crosstied Sheik, and he forced his nerves and muscles to relax. Suspicion licked at him, the clear memory of broad shoulders turned against him while Silas Dunn plotted with his henchmen to drive horses onto —

"Dead Horse Point. That's it!" Andy sprang up, galvanized into action. Hope rekindled. "Come on, Horse. We don't have time to waste."

Five minutes later, they were out of the valley and on their way. Andy's keen eyes didn't miss a sign, and a herd of wild horses being driven left plenty of them. Dusk overtook him and still he pushed on until darkness warned further travel could be disastrous.

He reluctantly made camp, but at first light, he had already stamped out the remains of his small fire and turned the mare onto the clearly marked trail. A passing thought that Reddy and the others would be leaving the Rocking A just about this time crossed his mind. His lips set in a grim line. He couldn't count on their help. Long before they reached the valley and tracked him, he'd be at the Point.

The day wore on, and his sense of urgency grew as well as a restless desire to push his mount beyond her strength. He resisted, and violet shadows lay long on the ground before he reached his destination. With the caution learned as a young lad on his own, especially when he worked on the Cross Z and kept his ears and eyes open to protect Columbine Ames, Andy dismounted when he saw the first flicker of campfire not far from the rim of the canyon. He tied his horse and belly-slid over the ground until he reached the fragile cover provided by a clump of greasewood. When no sound showed he'd been detected, he raised his head and peered through the stiff, thorny branches. He stiffened. Six men hunkered down around the fire. The smell of frying bacon and boiling coffee tantalized him, but after the first sniff, Andy forgot them. He concentrated on the men's faces, one by one.

Unless his eyes betrayed him, three of them were the men from the cafe who enthusiastically endorsed the wild horse drive. He dismissed them and studied the others but shook his head. Two of them could be any dark-visaged rider and might or might not be the holdup men who relieved Andy of his grub. The next moment, one laughed. Pleasant, appealing, the last time he'd heard it, a shot over his right shoulder followed.

Certainty replaced suspicion, and Andy shifted until he could examine the sixth man. Firelight fell on his uncovered face, reflected from his eyes. Weak with excitement, Andy looked straight into the odd, colorless eyes that had gleamed in campfire light months earlier. Any lingering doubt fled forever when Strange Eyes said eagerly, "Hey, Boss, lookee here," and held up a dead cottontail in the exact way he'd dangled Andy's saddlebags at their first meeting.

The cowboy's breath came faster, but cool reason prevailed. One against six meant defeat or bloodshed. Could he lie low until the roundup crew arrived tomorrow? He considered and rejected a dozen plans. First, he must locate Sheik and Chinq. Beyond that, he couldn't plan. He inched his way out of earshot and back to his horse. What if he could find Sheik? He must be tied. Andy's blood boiled at the probable treatment the big stallion had suffered through if captured. On the other hand, just maybe Sheik had been canny enough to keep his presence unknown to the men driving the horse herd, no mean feat for six riders.

Andy's heart leaped. In that event, his own job would be easier than stealing milk from a well-trained cow. If only he had Chinq instead of the mare, whose full capabilities he couldn't count on. "No use wishing for the moon," he muttered. "I have to make do with what I've got."

Tremendous curiosity filled him. Now that

he'd satisfied himself about the riders at the campfire, he'd take a gander at the narrow neck of land called Dead Horse Point. A tiny bit of light remained in the sky, just enough for him to make his way to the Point. He guided the mare forward. She acted willing enough, probably caught the scent of horse. It wouldn't matter if she whinnied. One horse among many wouldn't alarm the men at the fire.

In the last gleam of dusk, he saw what he expected. A band of mares, colts, and fillies milled on the thirty-yard-wide neck of land bounded on three sides by canyon. The fourth side boasted a crude fence formed of scraggly brush, lassoes, and a couple of crooked posts fashioned from stunted tree trunks.

Andy grunted and relief washed through him. That so-called fence might discourage mares and young horses from a breakout. Sheik would snort his disdain and leap it in a minute. So would Chinq. Obviously, they were not part of the herd.

He risked a low whistle. Some of the penned horses called back, then off to Andy's left, a familiar nicker sounded. He turned in that direction, spirits rising like the Colorado River in flood. "Chinq?" he called. "Sheik?"

Another nicker. A deeper whinny. A quick rush of hooves, and two horses came to him. The pitch blackness that had fallen couldn't disguise their sounds or the yelling that arose in the horse herders' camp.

"We have to get out of here," Andy told the horses. Leaving the Rocking A mare saddled, he leaped to Sheik's back, hoping the mare would follow the way Chinquapin did. "All right, Boy. Make tracks."

The stallion pranced. Andy gripped the bridle and began the strangest ride of his life. Without saddle or blanket, he pressed his legs to Sheik's sides and prayed the horse wouldn't step in a gopher hole in his wild flight. He heard Chinq and the other mare behind them and made no effort to halt the black until he knew they'd put enough distance between them and the Point so the men camped there couldn't track him in the dark. He also took the precaution, once stopped, to transfer the mare's saddle to Sheik and hobble and tie him. The taste of freedom in the stallion's journey back to the valley might have done irreparable harm to the breaking process. He couldn't chance having a determined horse nosing around the makeshift corral and triggering a panic that would rouse the captors.

Worn out by worry and the long, hard pursuit, Andy fell into a black, dreamless sleep. A wild scream brought him wide awake, and a terrifying sight greeted his unbelieving eyes. He started to leap to his feet. A rope sang through the air. A flicker of time later, he fell, jerked clean off his feet by the lasso. In a twinkling, he lay bound hand and foot, his gaze fixed on Sheik, held fast by a half-dozen ropes and trying to get out from under four men who pinned him to the ground.

"Watch out!" Andy's warning rang just in time. Strange Eyes, who knelt beside the black's head, jerked back, barely escaping Sheik's vicious bite.

His face darkened. "I'll teach you." He cracked the stallion across the nose and just missed losing a hand.

"Stop it!" The man who had bound Andy sprang toward the horse. "You'll make a killer out of him and Du— we don't want that."

Andy warmed to him despite the perilous circumstances. He recognized him as the thief with the pleasant laugh. "Thanks, Mister."

"Say, don't I know you?"

Andy nearly bit his tongue in two to keep back the accusation jammed behind his teeth. "You might," he substituted.

"Hey, you're that feller —"

"Forget it." Andy took a chance and cut off disclosures that could prove fatal. With a quick prayer for help, he asked, "Why the holdup? Watch your hand!" he yelled at Strange Eyes, who had turned his attention to Andy and carelessly leaned too close to the captive stallion.

"Mighty concerned about me, ain't you?" the man jeered.

"More concerned that you'll teach my horse to be scareder of men than he already is," Andy shot back.

"Your horse?" The thief's eyebrows nearly reached his hair. "I don't see no brand."

A sickening feeling attacked Andy. "His name's Sheik. I caught and broke him. He ain't never been ridden by anyone else, and he's mine, brand or no. I found him and his mares —"

"Stolen."

"Sure. Stallions steal mares." Andy twisted against the uncomfortable ropes that cut into his wrists and ankles until he could get into a sitting position. "Allen of the Rocking A and all the other ranchers who've lost mares to Sheik — *including Silas Dunn* — are on their way right now to the valley where I left the band. I aim to return the mares and dicker for the colts and fillies."

"Sure you are." Strange Eyes jumped to his feet, face ablaze. "You've no proof the horses are yours. There's six of us to swear we found them, which we did, freed them, and drove them onto the Point."

"And there's sixty or six hundred to swear they saw me ride Sheik in the Moab Independence Day race and win," Andy flashed back. "We hang horse thieves in Arizona. I don't know what you do with them here."

The enraged man raised a heavy booted foot to kick the tied cowboy, but the leader yelled and told him to lay off. "Fine kettle of rotten fish," he bawled. "Did you know this?" He whirled toward the three guilty-looking men from the cafe who shuffled and admitted they'd heard that a yellow-headed kid won the race.

Sensing a possible split that could only be in his favor, Andy goaded some more. He even managed a cheerful grin. "Getting so you can't trust no one these days. Not trying to tell you your business, but if I were you, I'd hightail it out of here before that roundup outfit rides in. No telling what Allen and his boys will do when they find me trussed up like a Christmas pig ready for the roasting."

The flicker in the leader's eyes showed

doubt, and Andy took heart. Sheik lay panting, temporarily defeated but still showing signs of fight.

"We ain't horse thieves," the leader protested. "We could have stole horses lots of times." He pointed his words with a significant look toward Chinquapin, who hovered close enough to see her incapacitated lord and master.

"I didn't think *you* were." Andy left it at that but couldn't resist adding, "What I know is you were hired by Silas Dunn to round up mustangs and drive them onto the Point, then build a corral and keep them there." He forestalled questions by tersely saying, "I heard Dunn and your three friends talking in Moab." His steady glance never left the leader.

The man turned to Dunn's representatives. "Pay up."

"What?" Their faces blackened with anger and surprise.

"Dunn's deal was to drive a herd to the Point, which we did. Me and my boys'll just take our money and vamoose."

Strange Eyes growled low in his throat, but the leader quelled him with a glance. "We ain't having any part in robbing this guy of his horse." He sent a contemptuous glance in his comrades' direction. "Dunn can kill his own snakes when he gets here. We stumbled on the valley, sent for you as agreed on, and made a long, hard drive. Fork over. Now!"

Andy secretly grinned at the results of the innocent-sounding comment. Dunn's men hastily conferred, then one pulled out a roll of bills and sullenly tossed it to the leader.

"Dunn won't like this," he shouted when the trio strode away, Strange Eyes protesting but obviously intimidated by his boss.

"Who cares?" A mellow laugh rang back to them, and the leader tossed the roll of bills. "Me and the boys are tired of Utah, anyway. Think we'll take us a little vacation and try somewhere else. Pickings around here are getting mighty slim."

Andy watched them ride out of sight, again thinking he could have liked the man if he hadn't been a thief and maybe worse. *What causes a fellow with a laugh like that to go bad?*

He didn't have time to consider it. The three men from town stood frowning down at him.

"What're we gonna do with him and the horse?" one asked.

"Leave him here and swear to Dunn he jumped us, tried to run us down with the stallion."

181

"Think it will hold water?" The third man looked skeptical.

"Why not? Any fool can see the horse's capable of killing a man if he took a notion."

"I don't like giving any horse a bad name," the first speaker complained. "Remember what happened to the black's daddy."

A pool of silence descended. Andy lay perfectly still. Sheik's future hung in the balance.

"Aw, why don't we just tell the truth?" the second man suggested. "We'll tell the boss the big, bad outlaws he hired roped and tied Sheik and his rider, then got cold feet and hightailed it out of here when they heard a bunch of ranchers and hands were on their way." He shot Andy a sharp glance. "Right, Cowboy?"

"That's the way it looked from here. 'Course, I ain't in much of a position to argue. How about untying me?"

"Hold your horses, and I don't mean Sheik. What's Dunn gonna do about those mares and colts and fillies?"

"Let him worry about them. I'm sick of this deal, anyway. I never figured on getting stuck with a band of mostly branded horses," the first man growled. "They were s'posed to be mustangs who belong to

anyone, not a passel of already owned nags."
He turned on his heel. "Count me out."

"Too late," one of his friends sang out. "A rider's coming and fast."

"*A* rider? Thought you said a whole outfit was heading this way," the first man accused. "What're you doing, trying to make fools out of us?"

Andy slowly shook his head. "They are. I don't know who'd be riding alone." Yet a sneaking suspicion that neither his nor Sheik's troubles were over sent dread through his bound body, and the closer the rider came, the louder the drum of hooves, the more he feared the unknown horseman bearing down on them as if Satan himself followed behind.

CHAPTER 11

"How about untying me?" Andy said again. "If our visitor proves a mite unfriendly, I'm pretty good in a scrap."

"Forget it. We can handle a single rider. Besides," he added when a lathered horse pounded around a rock outcropping and slid to a stop in front of them, "it's the boss."

Andy sagged against the ropes. Silas Dunn might be one tough hombre, but he didn't appear to be a killer. His relief proved short lived. The unpleasant smile and hatred in the broad-shouldered man told the hogtied cowboy he hadn't been forgiven for the matter of the saddle blanket. He decided to take the initiative. "Where's the rest of the outfit?" Andy demanded.

"Trailing toward the valley," Dunn gloated. "By the time they get here, my men and I'll have full claim to the horses on the Point."

"Is that so?" Andy set his jaw, hating the

advantage Dunn had over him because of the ropes. He expanded his muscles, relaxed them, and silently rejoiced when he felt them slacken. Left alone, he might work free.

"So you got Sheik." Dunn's eyes gleamed, and his face paled with greed. "Best horse I ever saw. Cullen, you should have sold him while you had the chance." He stepped from the saddle of the sorrel mare that no longer wore Andy's blanket and, shaking with excitement, walked toward Sheik. "I'll have him gelded and make him into the best saddle horse in the country."

Andy strained against his bonds. "Then you're the biggest fool in Utah," he hoarsely told the rancher. "Unless you want a poor-spirited nag, ashamed to hold his head up."

"He's right, Boss," one of the men put in. "I'm here to say I ain't gonna stand for any such thing."

"Me, neither," the others agreed.

"So, getting soft, huh? Just remember who put up the money for this deal."

"This deal, as you call it, is over," a cowhand snapped. "Those fancy outlaws you hired to drive the horses have took off. How are you going to take care of that bunch of animals on the Point without them . . . and us?" he added significantly.

Rage turned Dunn's face black. "You yellow-bellies," he bellowed. "I should have known you wouldn't have the stomach for an opportunity like this."

"You said it, Boss. But maybe you'll change your mind when you find out most of the mares are already wearing brands." The rider never budged an inch. "Unless you're considering changing brands, which ain't healthy in these parts. The owners aren't going to stand by with their hands in their pockets while you claim their horses."

"I can claim the colts and fillies."

"How?" Andy asked. "From what I hear, your men aren't willing to lie for you, and my word's better than yours. The ranchers have already learned from Allen who really found the herd."

Dunn speechlessly paced the ground, alternately glaring at Andy and his men and hurling invectives.

"That'll be about all," one finally said. "We got in this 'cause it sounded like an honest way to make some money. I'm dealing myself out now that it's beginning to stink, and I advise my pards to do the same." He backed off a step, then a knowledgeable look crossed his face. "On second thought, maybe we'd better stick around. I'd hate for this young feller to have an accident and then get blamed for it."

"You . . . you . . . cowards." Dunn frothed at the mouth and clenched his fists. With effort, he regained control. "I'll just have a look at the horses on the Point." He leaped into the sorrel mare's saddle, spurred her, and clattered off.

"Thanks, men." Andy let out a sigh of pent-up frustration. "I'd as soon face a wounded grizzly as be left alone with Dunn in this mood. Like you said, I'd hate to have an accident before the outfit gets here. Now, how about letting me up so I can free Sheik."

"Sure." The same rider who'd said he wouldn't stand for Sheik's being gelded produced a knife and cut Andy's bonds.

"Better stand back." Andy rubbed circulation back into his wrists and ankles and stepped toward Sheik, who lunged toward him but only succeeded in falling back because of the ropes. "He's never been handled rough except when I first caught and tamed him."

The men walked away a respectful distance.

"There, Boy. No one's going to hurt you," Andy soothed. Step by step, he came closer to the terrified animal. "Steady, now."

For a time, he didn't think the stallion

would let him touch him, but a lot of coaxing later, Andy laid his hand on the black's quivering neck. More quiet talk and the loosening of the ropes that still held, and Sheik stood free. He stood absolutely still for a moment, then shook his head as if coming out of a daze. The next instant he reared, catching Andy off guard.

The cowboy leaped aside but stumbled. Numbness from the tight ropes hadn't completely disappeared. It slowed his actions and made it impossible to keep his balance.

Sheik came down heavily, twisting sidewise in a desperate effort to avoid his owner, but a fraction of a second too late.

Andy, who had hit the ground and tried to roll out of the way, felt a blow to his temple before everything went black.

An eternity later, he roused enough to hear loud shouting and the rolling thunder of many pounding hooves. He tried to struggle out of the terrible darkness clutching at him but could barely give a low moan. His eyelids stayed glued shut, and his weary brain refused to think. An effort to raise his head plummeted him fathoms deep into the smothering night.

After the outfit had ridden away after Andy

Cullen, Linnet Allen spent most of her waking hours aimlessly strolling from house to corral or sitting on the wide porch, watching the road. She'd hidden and watched wide eyed during her uncle's discussion with the ranchers and cowboys who rode in at George's summons. Keen to spot the unusual, Linnet had also caught the quick glance around and shifty way a certain broad-shouldered man's colorless gaze swept the crowded room. In the vernacular of Mrs. Salt, she'd wager anything the man was Silas Dunn. Secure in her hiding place, she shivered. Imagine having that person coming to court a young girl! Unthinkable. The contrast of Andy Cullen's laughing but respectful attitude brought a rich blush to the eavesdropping girl.

After a lot of haranguing, and hemming and hawing on Dunn's part, mostly protesting the fact that the colts and fillies belonged to their finder, the whole bunch of them rode off. Linnet burst from seclusion and ran to the front porch, wondering if the fact that Reddy, Tommy, and Charlie rode grouped at the rear with their heads turned in Silas Dunn's direction held any significance.

"Child, you've been staring down that trail all day," Mrs. Salt complained. "It's been only a couple of days. Give them time."

Linnet turned toward her. "I can't help feeling something is wrong." Even though her good friend and substitute mother pooh-poohed the idea, the young woman couldn't shake the feeling of dread until the morning of the third day following the outfit's departure when she saw a dust cloud far down the road in the direction from which she knew the men would return.

"Mrs. Salt, the men are coming!" Linnet left the porch and hurried down the steps and across the wide space toward the corral, intending to open the gate for the herd of horses. Something in the slow progress of a band of riders far smaller than she'd expected halted her. "Why . . . ?"

Fear lent speed to her feet. She changed direction and flew over the uneven ground toward the snail-paced caravan. Her blue eyes, which had become accustomed to long distances in her time on the Rocking A, widened, and a fresh spurt of terror sped through her when she saw that the chestnut mare called Chinquapin carried a huddled, motionless figure tied in the saddle.

"Father? Uncle George?" Her piercing cry reached the riders before she did.

"They're all right," Reddy Hode called back. "It's Cullen."

A pang went through her. The relief she expected to feel didn't materialize. She ran faster and arrived at the somber-faced bunch. "What happened?" She stared at the quiet figure.

"I'll tell you later, Miss Allen. Tommy, go tell Mrs. Salt to have a bed ready."

"Is he . . . dead?" Linnet managed to gasp. Her heart pounded more from fear than exertion, and she turned back toward the house and the racing horseman.

"Naw, but he needs help. Charlie's already ridden to Moab for the doctor," Reddy evaded.

"Where are Father and Uncle George?"

Hode's eyes glittered. "Rounding up the horses." His lips set with the firmness of a steel trap clicking shut, and Linnet knew she'd hear no more for the moment.

She looked at the dust-stained, quiet figure on the mare he loved. Quick tears crept into her eyes. She scolded herself for them. The last thing anyone needed was a sissy tenderfoot getting in the way. The thought braced her, and after Mrs. Salt and Reddy expertly undressed Andy and put him to bed in a first-floor room, she peeped in.

His fine hands lay curiously still on the turned-back, spotless white sheet. A crisp

191

bandage had replaced the bloodstained one binding his head.

Again she fought tears, then hastened out of the sickroom at Mrs. Salt's peremptory motion and whispered, "All we can do's to wait for Doc." Reddy and Tommy lounged on the front porch but straightened to attention and doffed their hats when she stepped outside.

"Tell me everything." She sank into a rocker.

Reddy took the lead. His eyes flashed when he said, "We've put together bits and pieces. When we got to the hidden valley Cullen described, it lay open and empty." His face darkened. "Shoulda kept a better eye on Dunn." He sounded disgruntled.

"Yeah." Tommy shifted his weight from one foot to the other. "He ducked out on us somewhere between here and the valley, probably when we had to ride single file to get around some rocks next to the trail."

Reddy took up the story again. "I had a hunch and said so. The boss agreed, and we hightailed it for Dead Horse Point. Found a . . . a mess. Cullen lying on the ground with blood pouring out of his head. Three riders from the Bar D standing over him, and Dunn just sliding from the saddle."

"Did the men *shoot* Andy?" Rage such as

she had never before felt brought Linnet out of the rocker and to her feet.

"Naw. 'Cording to the men, they and some others, whose names they kept to themselves, had driven the horses to the Point, split over the deal going sour, and the others rode off, not wanting to meet us when we got there."

"But what happened to Andy?" Linnet demanded.

"I'm getting to that. Sheik and his lady friend, Chinquapin, had followed the horse herd. So had Cullen, who rounded up his horses and put some distance between. Well, the Bar D men ran across them and tied up Cullen *and* Sheik." His clear face flushed, and the corners of his mouth turned down. "Just about scared the stallion to death. When Cullen set him free, he started pitching, and when he came down, his foot knocked Cullen square in the head."

Tommy put in, "Your uncle roared, and some of us were all for running Dunn out of the country. Your daddy said to just let him take a couple of mares wearing his brand and let him go 'cause nothing could be proved against him."

A satisfied smile crawled across Reddy's face. "Dunn won't be pulling any crooked deals for awhile, at least." His grin died.

"We talked about sending for a wagon, but Cullen came to long enough to mumble he could ride, so we tied him in the saddle after patching him up until his head looked like one of those quilts Mrs. Salt makes."

"Father and Uncle George should have come with him," Linnet said in an accusing tone.

"No need for that. They figured Cullen'd rather have them bring in the herd." Reddy's gaze wavered.

"What aren't you telling me?" Linnet asked.

He reddened and again avoided her direct gaze.

"Aw, she d'serves to know," Tommy exploded.

"Sheik took off like a scared jackrabbit in front of a pack of wolves." Reddy squirmed. "Cullen's mare went with him but couldn't keep up. We caught her while the boss patched Cullen's head." He heaved a great sigh. "One of the reasons the boss decided to keep most of the outfit and drive the horses back here is he figured Sheik ain't gonna take kindly to losing his herd."

"What if he doesn't come?" Linnet thought of the magnificent horse who had so easily cleared her body in one giant leap.

"I reckon it would 'most break Cullen's

heart," Reddy admitted.

"You said that was one of the reasons?" She caught the meaningful look the hands exchanged.

"The colts and fillies aren't branded. If left on the Point, what's to prevent Dunn from showing up after we're gone and burning the Bar D on them?" Reddy shot back.

"Life sure wasn't like this in Boston."

Hode's keen eyes softened. "But you wouldn't trade it, would you? This here place has done healed you. Miss Allen, you sure couldn't have come running to meet us when you first got here."

With a quick prayer for guidance and the right words, Linnet slowly said, "No, I never want to go back, but as much as I've learned to love Utah Territory and the Rocking A, I can't thank them for my health . . . and life." She swallowed hard and felt tears mist her lashes. The cowboys maintained a sympathetic silence. "It's God who healed me."

"No arguing with that," Reddy gruffly said, and Tommy nodded. Linnet thought of what Mrs. Salt had said about the outfit's regard for her. *It's good for them to have someone to admire and hold high. . . . The way you live your life as a witness for the Lord may be making a far deeper impression . . . than any of us know.*

It felt like weeks before the capable doctor who Linnet remembered from her brief encounter arrived in a buggy, escorted by Charlie Moore. He and Mrs. Salt closeted themselves for a long time with the still unconscious cowboy. The doctor had questioned the hands, and according to Charlie, "Had a pure conniption fit," when he found out Cullen had been put on a horse and packed back to the ranch house. Charlie looked awed. "Never knew a man could get so mad, and I've seen plenty of upset fellers." Now he joined Linnet and his two friends on the porch and waited.

Mrs. Salt came out, a troubled look on her face and in her blue eyes. "Wish Mr. Allen were here. Doc says he has to operate; he thinks there's a bone pressing where it isn't supposed to." Her keen gaze traveled from face to face. "I'll help, but he needs one other person. Who's it going to be?"

Reddy turned pale under his tan; Charlie and Tommy just stared. Linnet felt her heart bounce. Sweat sprang to her face. Her hands turned icy. "I'll help."

A wave of protest rang from the cowboys, but she shook her head. "His riding saved me. I want to help . . . if I don't have to look at what's happening." Nausea at the idea attacked her.

"What would Mr. Judd say?" Mrs. Salt expostulated.

"He'd say I must do anything I can to help." The thought steadied her. "Just tell me what to do."

"Get into the oldest, plainest dress you own. On second thought, I'll get you something." She hustled the girl to her room, dug into a pile of clothes she said she'd been keeping for rags, waited while Linnet got into them, then pulled her hair back, fashioned a cap from a dish towel, and led her to the sick room.

"Miss Allen, are you fit for this?" the doctor sternly asked. "I don't want to move him any more . . . even to a table. This means you'll have to bend until your back aches. Mrs. Salt knows enough about my instruments to hand them to me, but I need you to hold the cowboy's head still. I can't be responsible for what happens if he moves his head."

" 'I can do all things through Christ which strengtheneth me.' " The words sprang unbidden from her lips and settled into her trembling, fearful heart. A wellspring of courage, beyond anything she had ever known, steadied her hands and voice, and her mind repeated the familiar words again and again.

Before the doctor directed Mrs. Salt on how to give the anesthetic, he pressed on a spot above the patient's temple. From the depths of unconsciousness came a moan, and the doctor grunted with satisfaction. "Just as I thought."

Every time Linnet knew she could not stay in the rigid position and hold Andy's head steady, she bit her lip, closed her eyes, and prayed — for the doctor, for Mrs. Salt, for herself. But most of all for the valiant young cowboy who, in their few short meetings, had somehow woven himself into the fabric of her life. If anyone had told her in the spring that she would be a crucial part of helping to save a man's life, how she would have laughed. A prayer of thankfulness rose to her lips and hovered over her during the rest of the operation. An eternity later, the operation ended.

"Well done, Lass." The doctor glanced at her. "Are you all right?"

She straightened her back, weary from bending. The room spun. "I . . . I think so."

He pushed her into a chair and told her to hold her head between her knees. The rush of blood to her brain cleared away the dizziness. "Thank you. Will he be all right?"

"He's young, strong. We took care of the problem. I predict that by fall he will be back riding wild broncs." The doctor's eyes twinkled. "In the meantime, he can enjoy a soft bed, Mrs. Salt's good food, and a pretty nurse."

Linnet felt herself flush; gladness filled her. "Thank God."

"I always do." He beetled his brows at her and began helping Mrs. Salt clean up. "Go on outside into the fresh air."

Linnet stumbled from fatigue when she stepped over the doorsill onto the porch. Three guilt-stricken faces greeted her.

"Aw, you're all in." Reddy pushed a chair forward. "We're a bunch of skunks for letting you do it."

"I had no choice." She leaned her head back against the chair top.

"I reckon you didn't, at that. How is he?"

Weariness dropped like a diver into deep water. "He's alive, sleeping naturally, and Doc says he will be okay."

Concern gave way to joshing. Linnet realized it for what it was: the cowboys' way of relieving their worries and frustration at being helpless to aid a fallen companion.

"If you don't need us, we'll ride back out and help bring the herd in," Reddy told her.

"Since we ain't lucky enough to live in bed and have you fetch and carry for us."

Banners of red flew in her face. "Go ahead, boys. The more of you there are, the sooner Father will come." She held her eyes wide open to hide the tears that persisted in crowding up at the thought of her father and his strength that she needed. After the trio left, she let the tears spill, then wiped her face and ran upstairs to bathe and change into a fresh outfit.

At Linnet's insistence, Mrs. Salt reluctantly consented to let her take part of the night watch over the patient. Doc had propped pillows on both sides of his head and warned of the need for them to remain in place.

Heart pounding, Linnet seated herself near the bed. A kerosene lamp, turned down until it gave only the faintest yellow glow, cast grotesque shadows on the walls. The even breathing of the patient told his nurse that all was well. Hours later, long after Mrs. Salt had promised to relieve her, Linnet still sat there. The worthy woman must have failed to waken. It didn't matter. Andy hadn't roused.

Contradictory to the thought, a few minutes later, he stirred and tried to turn his head, although his eyes stayed shut. Linnet slipped to her knees and placed a cool hand on his brow. "Don't try to move. You were hurt, but you're going to be all right, thanks to God. Just rest." Her soothing voice went on and on, and he again slept, but when she removed her hand, he turned restless. She replaced it, and he grew quiet, with her still on her knees beside his bed.

For two days they watched him continuously. The second night he talked incoherently, but Linnet caught enough words about "pretty little girl" and "Now, Sheik!" to turn fiery red in the faint light.

"Lord, don't let her die."

She froze at her patient's first complete sentence and wiped sweat from his face. His next words turned her from cold to hot, though she had to bend close to hear them.

"She'll never look at me, Lord, but I love her."

CHAPTER 12

The next day, the Rocking A riders came home minus Sheik's stolen mares, claimed and driven off by their owners, but with a passel of unbranded stock. Until Andy Cullen regained health and chose which horses to keep and which to sell, the herd would remain intact in the pasture that Sheik and Chinquapin had briefly inhabited on the fateful night such a short time ago.

Linnet formed the habit of visiting the pasture whenever she could, that is, when Mrs. Salt chased her away from the nursing duties she had gladly taken on. Linnet told her father, "I never dreamed what was in me. I hated helping Doc, but I did it." Her blue eyes sparkled; her face glowed. "I also didn't know how easy learning to ride would be."

He looked at her radiant face. "Thank God" was all he could say.

Sadie, the gentle white mare assigned to

Linnet, took Linnet on her back as easily as she took sugar and carrots from the hands that had lost some of their delicateness but gained beauty from serving others. The pastured horses learned to know Linnet's call and would come to the fence when she and Sadie arrived. Linnet's eyes glistened at their wild charm, yet most often her gaze would stray to the chestnut mare, Chinquapin, and a slow smile would light up her face. Never in the time following Andy Cullen's return to consciousness had he in word or deed expressed the love he had revealed, yet Linnet's secret knowledge filled her heart, and an answering feeling began. While family and outfit rejoiced over her return to health, she hugged to herself dreams of the future and a devoted cowboy who definitely did not have bowlegs!

Andy daily gained strength; so did Linnet. He chafed under the doctor's restrictions to rest and not take chances; she rode and traded her white skin for a clear tan tinged with red from sun and wind. She and Andy talked about many things: Sheik, Andy's lonely years since his parents died, Linnet's attempt to be courageous in the face of impending death. Gradually, their conversations grew more serious, and they spoke of God.

"Andy," she said one sunny afternoon from the wide porch that overlooked the corrals and range, bathed in summer haze. "You're a Christian, aren't you?" She held her breath, instinctively realizing his answer could make a vast difference in her future.

"I asked the Lord to be my Trailmate, my Pard, after I met Smokey and Joel and the others," he told her. A note of doubt crept into his voice. "I guess that makes me a Christian."

Linnet stumbled for words. "Do you pray?"

"I talk to Him, man to Man, the way I'd talk to Smokey, and He's the Best Friend I ever had, even better than Columbine." He'd long since told of his boyish regard for the girl he considered far above him. "Is that enough?"

Again she sought for just the right thing to say. On impulse, she laid one hand over his that lay on the rocker arm next to her. "I think it's grand that you share that kind of feeling. It's important, though, to know and accept Jesus as your personal Savior. He died in our place so we could have everlasting life."

Andy turned his palm up and gently squeezed her fingers. "Linnet, I would never have dared ask Him to take me on as His pard if Columbine and Smokey hadn't showed me how much God loved a plain old cowpoke and sinner like me," he said huskily.

Glad tears pushed against the girl's eyes. She slipped her hand from his and smiled mistily. "That makes me . . . and Him . . . very happy."

Neither noticed that in that precious moment, Andy, for the very first time, had called her Linnet instead of Miss Allen. Afterwards, she blushed rosy red, and the strong but respectful touch of his work-hardened fingers lingered.

After she went inside, Andy stared unseeingly across the Rocking A he had come to love second only to his cherished Arizona Territory. Linnet's light touch felt burned into his palm. A tide of warmth rose within him, and he thought of the look in her blue eyes when she smiled and said he had made her happy. He pondered, trying to decide whether she'd have felt the same for anyone who loved the Master or if part of the joy was because Andy Cullen hadn't disappointed her.

The longing to be astride a good horse and ride until he felt ready to drop from the saddle assailed him, and his heart leaped. A few more days, Doc had said on his last flying visit. Yet regret blended with the exultation. Once he returned to riding, roping, and rounding up, he'd have little opportunity to see Linnet. No more magical hours of sharing and getting to know each other in the way they had done during his convalescence.

Andy deliberately turned his thoughts elsewhere. *Where was Sheik?* A few times during the weeks he'd been laid up, uncertain reports of a black stallion seen from a distance created interest, but the riders couldn't identify the horse as Sheik. If the horse had visited his family, no sign showed. The thoughtful cowboy wholeheartedly believed he had not. Chinquapin remained in the pasture, more or less content. A couple of times Reddy Hode had driven Andy in the contraption and patiently waited while the Arizona hand petted his mare and took stock of the rest of the horses. The most recent visit had resulted in Andy's pointing out what colts and fillies he wanted to keep. George and Judd Allen put in a bid for the rest of them, and Andy's nest egg made his eyes pop wide open.

"Remember what I said," George told him. "There's plenty of space on the Rocking A, and I wouldn't mind selling you enough to get you started on a little spread of your own."

Andy thought it over. His long-held visions of a cabin and family danced in his mind, but this time he could see the wife who stood in the doorway to welcome him home. She looked amazingly like Linnet Allen.

"No hurry making up your mind," George said kindly.

Andy suspected those shrewd eyes saw clear to the bottom of his newest rider's boots, and he glanced away from the scrutiny.

Now he restlessly stirred and turned to his Trailmate and Savior. "Lord, I reckon if she . . . she cares, I'll stay. If not . . ." His voice trailed off. Where would he go if Linnet didn't care? Beyond recapturing Sheik, he had no ambitions, no desire to return to wild horse hunting. The only reason he'd ever begun to chase mustangs was because of the wild black stallion. Andy heaved a great sigh, then, with the philosophy of the range to deal with one day at a time, he left the future where it belonged — in his Creator's hands.

Fall came stealing on leaf-strewn winds. Peace reigned on the Rocking A, and business went on as usual. Back in the saddle,

Andy caught himself peering as far ahead as he could see, no matter where he rode. He discovered that Chinquapin did the same. An obstruction rose to the rider's throat. "Miss him, don't you, Girl?"

Chinq turned her head and observed him with soft eyes, then whinnied and resumed her scanning of the horizon.

Andy finished his day's work, rode back to the ranch, cleaned up, and parked on his bed in the bunkhouse. Reddy, Tommy, and Charlie dragged in, along with a half-dozen other cowhands. Dirty and sullen, they scarcely resembled the merry outfit that argued and played tricks but loyally refused to allow anyone outside the Rocking A to make disparaging comments.

"What's wrong, boys?" Andy asked.

"Aw, you tell him. I can't." Reddy threw his hat on the floor and glowered.

"I'm too mad to talk," Charlie added and flung himself into a chair. "Tommy, you spill the news."

Andy stood up, feeling that whatever was coming required him to be on his feet. "Rustlers haven't stolen horses or cattle, have they?"

"Worse," Reddy ground out. He wiped his sweaty face with a soiled neckerchief.

"Lin— Miss Allen? She's all right?" Andy

felt a primitive urge to throttle Reddy and get to the truth.

"She's fine. This deal don't concern the Rocking A 'cept it's so dirty, it's a slap in the face to any decent cowpoke." Reddy straightened from his dispirited slouch. To Andy's amazement, great drops stood on the other's contorted face.

"Reddy, what is it?"

The cowboy mopped at his face again; hatred shone from his eyes. "That skunk Dunn's pulled the rottenest trick ever heard of. It's gonna go down in Utah history as the blackest, meanest thing that could happen."

He paused and, in broken sentences, told the story. "For awhile after that time with Sheik, Dunn laid low, as you all know. Then kinda quietlike, he took up being what he is again. He rounded up the worst men he could find . . . the way I hear it, all his good riders walked out on him after what he did with Sheik."

Andy's nerves screamed. Would Reddy never get the story told?

"Anyhow, Dunn and his outfit went ahead with another horse drive. Sheik ain't the only stallion on the range with a herd of mares and young horses, just the best. Well, Dunn found a wild band. He succeeded in driving them onto Dead Horse Point, same as before." Pain twisted his face.

"What happened?"

Reddy stared into his eyes, but Andy had a feeling his pard was seeing a long line of horses instead. "Dunn and his men half broke the best of the lot, and you can bet how they did it."

Andy flinched, remembering the steel-like grip of some horse breakers he'd known. "It's a pure shame, but that's how a lot of them break horses," he offered.

"That ain't the worst of it," Tommy put in ominously.

A chill ran through Andy, and he jerked as if hit.

Reddy went on. "They drove off all the animals fit to sell and left the broomtails on Dead Horse Point. According to the story Dunn's giving out, the gate they put up was s'posed to be left open so the horses they left could find their way off the Point and back to the open range."

"So?" Andy braced himself.

"So somehow . . ." Reddy's gaze bored into him. "Somehow, no one knows or at least ain't telling, the gate stayed shut."

Andy felt the blood drain from his face, and he took a step back, hating the outcome of the story he already knew.

Reddy made a sound like a sob. "Those broomtails died of thirst, right there within sight of the Colorado River two thousand feet down from where they stood." He turned on his heel and bolted out of the bunkhouse.

The silence of compassion for suffering animals fell. Every cowboy there would shoot down a wild beast in time of danger or put a wounded animal out of its misery. But to leave horses, no matter how poor they might be, corralled on a rock promontory in the hot sun with no water transgressed every law of man and God.

Andy stepped outside and spotted Reddy standing by the corral, his shoulders drooping. He walked over and laid an arm across Reddy's back but said nothing until a new thought caused him to ask, "Does the boss know?"

"Yeah. He told us. For two bits, I'd go call Dunn out." A white line formed around his mouth.

"You don't need to, Reddy. A man has to pay for what he does. Besides, we don't know for sure who shut the gate or who didn't open it when he was supposed to."

"Yeah," Reddy said again. His muscles rippled, then relaxed. "Andy, how come God lets two-legged varmints like Dunn ride around the range pulling shady deals like this one?"

"From what I've seen of Dunn, I'd say Satan's bossing his life right now, not God."

"You sure hit it square between the eyes." The cowboy walked off without looking back, leaving Andy wondering if the seed he'd been able to plant would ever take root and grow.

Just before dusk, Andy, on his way to the bunkhouse, passed the wide front porch of the ranch house.

"Andy?" a soft voice called. The patter of feet on boards in a quick rush brought a young woman dressed in white to the top step. "Do you have time to talk?"

He heard tears in her voice and passionately longed to comfort her. His boot heels sounded loud on the steps, and he leaned against a porch post and looked down into her face, shadowed by falling night until her eyes turned dark and mysterious in her pale face.

"Is it true?" she whispered. Her hands clutched his two arms.

Andy suspected that, in her agitation, she didn't realize what she was doing. He couldn't say the same for himself. The touch of her hands sent love and longing through him. "Yes," he told her.

"Dear God, I'd hoped it was a rumor." Her hands dropped, then swept up to cover her face.

Scarcely conscious of his actions and stirred to the depths, he wrapped his arms around her and held her trembling body close. A start went through her before Linnet bowed her head against his chest and wept. In the few moments before she pulled back a little but not free, the last of Andy's boyhood vanished forever, replaced by manhood's strength and the need to care for his womenfolk.

"I . . . I'm sorry." She tilted her head back. Her white face blurred. "I —"

Nothing on earth could have kept Andy from lowering his head until his lips met and clung to hers for little more than a heartbeat. The next instant, he tore free. "Linnet, Sweetheart —"

"Lass, are you out here?"

With a low, incoherent cry, Andy ran down the steps and into the night, running away from the consequences of his actions as well as from Linnet and her uncle. Had he ruined his hope of heaven on earth with that kiss? Yet try as he would, Andy could not regret it. The soft pressure of lips he knew had been unkissed remained.

213

Unwilling to endure the endless bunk-house chafing, the distraught cowboy turned toward the corral. Chinquapin no longer roamed in the pasture but stayed closer to the ranch to be more accessible. Andy snatched blanket and saddle from their place in the barn, quickly saddled her, and rode away, pursued by memories.

Hours later he returned, cared for his mare, and crept noiselessly into the bunk-house, weary from the night ride and able to sleep the few remaining hours until morning.

His heart thudded when Reddy, who had gone out first, shoved the bunkhouse door open and yelled, "Hey, Cullen. Boss wants you."

It could mean only one thing. Linnet must have told her uncle, perhaps her father, of the moment on the porch. Andy considered just stuffing spare clothes into his bedroll and riding out. He could send for the money Allen owed him later. It would save embarrassment all around.

Coward, an inner voice accused. *Be a man and take your medicine.*

He threw back his head and marched to the main house like a gaily caparisoned Arabian on parade.

A court of four awaited him on the porch:

Linnet, eyes wide; Mrs. Salt, arms folded across her enveloping apron; George and Judd Allen, who grew more alike every day.

"You wanted me, Boss?" Some of the old insouciance returned to settle Andy down.

"My niece has something to say to you," George Allen boomed.

"Miss Allen?" Andy turned toward her, waiting for his sentence, reveling in her loveliness as she stood there wrapped in a wooly, white shawl against the early morning chill.

Eyes like twin stars looked straight into Andy's brown ones. "Andy, I thought a lot last night after we . . . we talked." A rich blush turned her the same rosy hue as the clouds touched by the rising sun. "If Silas Dunn is out catching wild horses, shouldn't you go find Sheik before that awful man gets him?"

The cowboy's lower jaw dropped. It was the last thing he'd expected.

Linnet rushed on. "Father and Uncle George agree. So does Mrs. Salt." An indescribable look crept into her face, one that needed to be examined in private.

"I'd give anything to go." Andy wheeled toward his employers.

"Take as much time as you need," George Allen gruffly told him. Understanding shone in his eyes. "I remember after Sheik's daddy stole my mare, I spent a lot of days and nights trying to get her back."

If only he could have a moment with Linnet! Yet even if he did, what could he say? Andy hid a small sigh and looked at each of the porch's occupants in turn. "I'm beholden." The quaint expression said what he could not.

"Hurry back, Andy. God go with you." Linnet's benediction rested on him like a poncho, and forty-five minutes later, the bemused cowboy mounted Chinquapin and rode away, remembering the smile on the lips he had kissed and the freedom from condemnation in her eyes. He thanked God he hadn't offended her.

Following a cold trail proved fruitless. Andy spent two weeks tracking down rumors, replenished his supplies at Moab, and went out again. Nights grew chill, and still he found no trace of Sheik. Had Sheik left southeastern Utah and ranged elsewhere, starting over, stealing mares, and building a new herd? Andy shuddered at the thought. It meant he might never again see the black stallion he loved.

Finally, encroaching winter drove him back to the Rocking A. Only the warmth of

Linnet Allen's welcome saved him from despair. He'd prayed to find Sheik, and for some reason, the Lord hadn't answered. Or maybe, like Linnet pointed out, God was saying no.

Winter came, warmed and sweetened for Andy by the eastern young woman daily becoming more robust and western. Just before Christmas, he inveigled her into taking a ride. She'd long since graduated from Sadie and often rode Chinq, while Andy straddled whatever horse he fancied. On a rise of land that overlooked the Rocking A, Andy halted and courteously helped the bundled-up girl out of the saddle. He pointed west.

"In the spring, I'll be building a cabin there," he softly told her. "Linnet, will you be my wife and live there with me?"

Straight as a homing pigeon, she came into his arms and turned her face up for his kiss. "Andy Cullen, I'll be proud to be your wife."

Not until the cold day penetrated their warm garments did they leave the spot that would forever be special in memory and the scene of many visits in their life together.

Warm congratulations poured over them when they announced their news to the Rocking A. Andy best remembered Reddy

Hode's drawl, "Well, if I couldn't marry her, I'd as soon have you get her as anyone I know."

Spring came with an abundance of tiny desert flowers. A few days before the wedding date, Linnet found Andy standing on the porch, eyes turned toward the distant canyon country. The expression on his face when he glanced at her brought a rush of love and poignancy. She put her arms around him and said nothing, knowing he hadn't forgotten the magnificent black stallion unheard of during all these long months.

"Shall we visit our new home?" she suggested.

Andy nodded. "I wouldn't have believed how skilled the outfit would turn out to be in raising our cabin," he marveled. It stood on a ridge not far away, with a view that took a man's breath away. Barn, large corral, and space for a bunkhouse when needed sometime in the future, the snug spread offered a haven for the couple so soon to be man and wife.

"How does Chinq like her new home?" Linnet asked just before they reached their destination. Her gaze turned from the corral where the faithful mare stood a little apart from the younger horses.

He didn't answer.

She turned back. "Why, where did —" Linnet never finished her question.

A shrill whistle cut the air, followed by a whinny, then the neighing of the horses in the corral. A drooping, dusty horse stood outside the bars, nose extended to a chestnut mare inside.

Andy couldn't move. He whistled.

The strange horse turned and slowly came toward him.

With a wild yell, the cowboy ran toward the limping horse. "Sheik, old boy." He wrapped his fingers in the coarse mane. Tears burned his eyelids. "You old prodigal, where have you been?" Andy tore free and examined the weary black, the lame leg last of all. He whooped again when he found a sharp stone securely wedged in the hoof. Thin and worn he might be, but Sheik was whole, and he had come home.

"I guess we'll never know," he told Linnet after he fed, watered, and rubbed Sheik down. "What's important is, he's back. I opened the corral gate, and he trotted in like he'd lived there forever." He ruefully added, "I hated to leave him for the night, but in just a few days . . . Linnet, it means so much more that Sheik chose to come

219

than if I'd just found him and brought him home." He swallowed hard. "I can't help thinking it's like with God. If He hogtied us and dragged us kicking and screaming, would we ever love Him? Ump-umm. Instead, He gives us all the rope we need. If we're smart, like Sheik, when we get to the end of it, we come back to where we belong."

Andy looked across the top of her head in the direction of Dead Horse Point. A pang rushed through him for the broomtails that had become captives of the canyon. He thought of pardners, trapped by sin, helpless as the penned horses. *Lord, thank You for freeing me,* he silently prayed. *If You can use this plain old cowboy to help round up others, I'll do it.*

Keenly aware of God's love, mightier than creation itself, Andy stood for a long time, the world in his arms, the hope of heaven in his soul. Like Sheik, the bent and weary prodigal, the restless, drifting rider had found where he belonged.

Dear Readers,

I hope you enjoy reading *Captives of the Canyon,* the last title in the Frontier Brides collection, as much as I enjoyed writing it. My parents had a deep love for reading and western history. They passed it on to my brothers and me. One Christmas during hard times Mom splurged and bought Dad twenty Zane Grey books. The $14. gift provided many happy hours reading by kerosene lamp light.

After World War 2 ended and money wasn't so tight, we camped all over the western states and saw places we already knew from Zane Grey's accurate descriptions. Those trips strengthened my desire to write western novels "someday."

"Someday" came years later when in 1977 I felt called to walk off my government job and write full-time. Now, with six million copies of my 140+ "Books You Can Trust" sold, I marvel. God chose an ordinary logger's daughter to help make the world a better place by providing inspirational reading.

May the FRONTIER BRIDES series bring

a smile, a tear, inspiration, and hope to each of you.

In His Service,
Colleen L. Reece